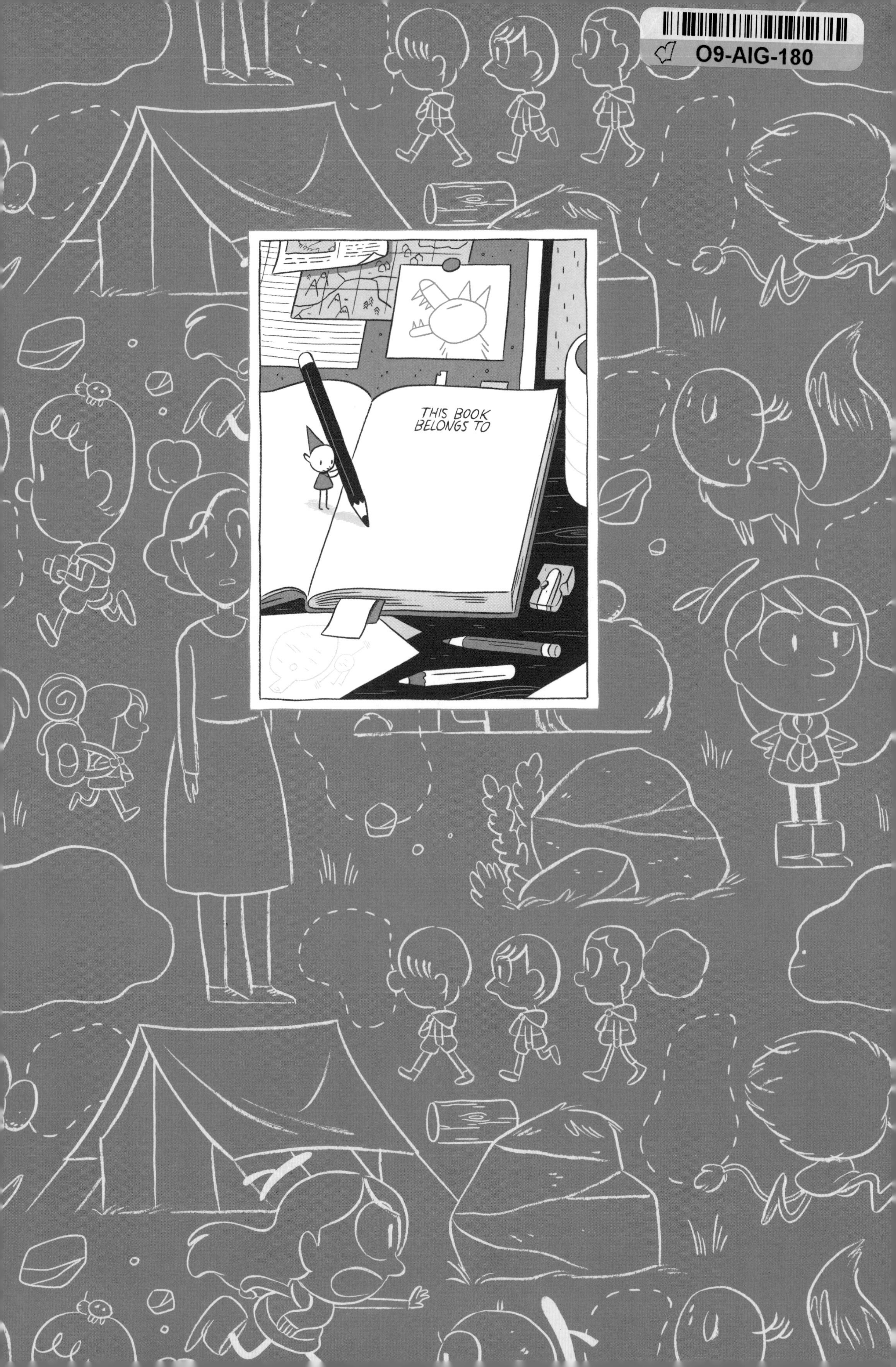
THIS BOOK
BELONGS TO

THANKS TO SAM, ALEX AND EVERYONE AT NOBROW, JON MCNAUGHT, JUTTA HARMS, ADAM MUTO AND ESPECIALLY TO PHILIPPA RICE, AMELIA PEARSON, MUM, DAD, MY FAMILY AND FRIENDS FOR THEIR ENDLESS SUPPORT AND UNDERSTANDING.

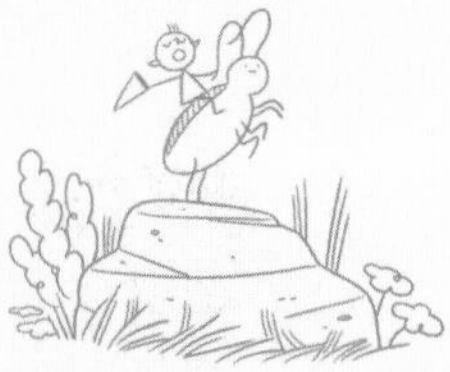



THIS IS A THIRD EDITION. FIRST PUBLISHED IN 2014.



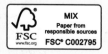

PUBLISHED BY FLYING EYE BOOKS, AN IMPRINT OF NOBROW LTD.
27 WESTGATE STREET, LONDON, E8 3RL
PUBLISHED IN THE US BY NOBROW (US) INC.

PRINTED IN LATVIA ON FSC® CERTIFIED PAPER
ISBN: 978-1-909263-18-5

MIX
Paper from responsible sources
FSC® C002795

ORDER FROM WWW.FLYINGEYEBOOKS.COM

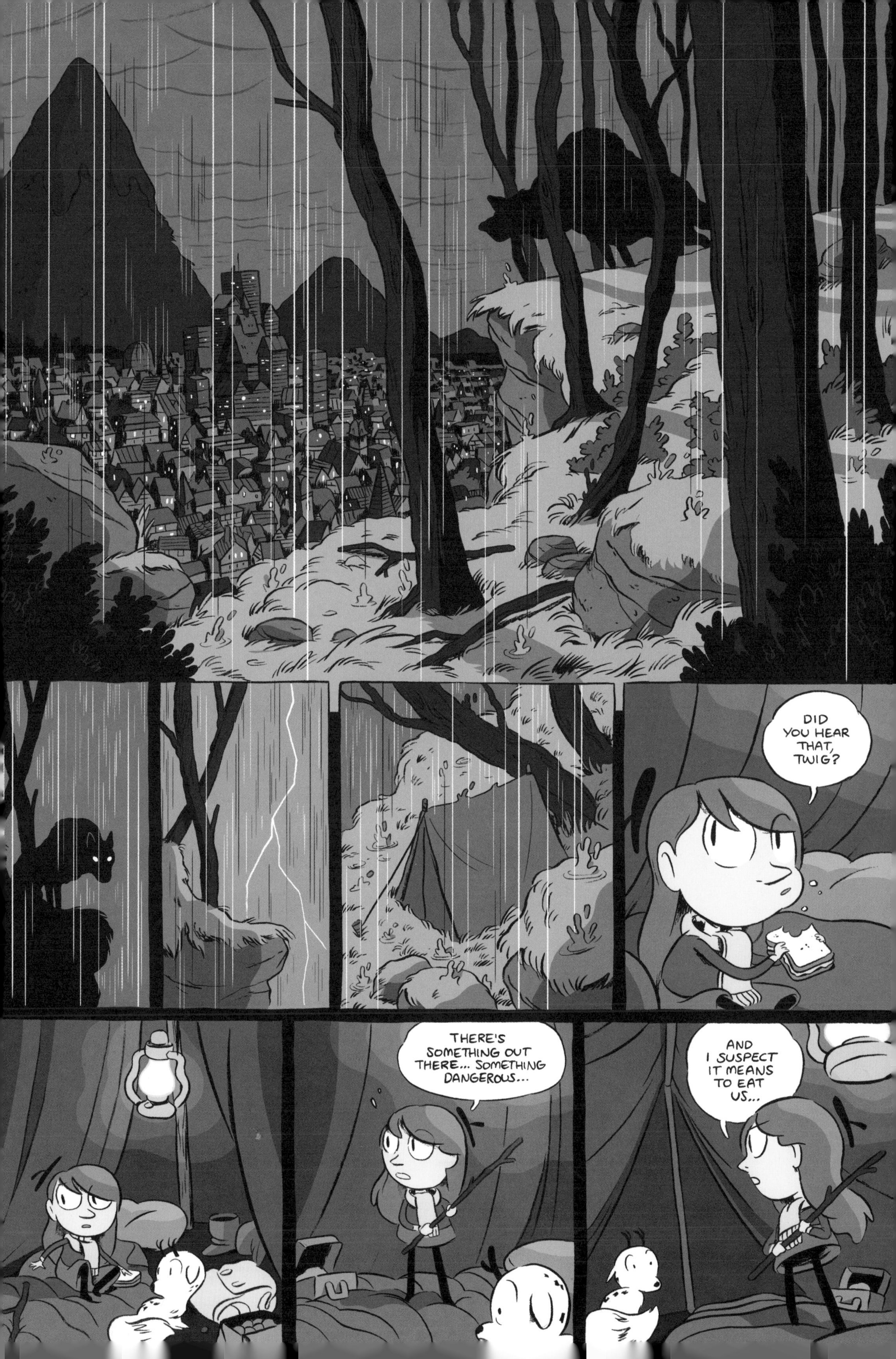
DID YOU HEAR THAT, TWIG?
THERE'S SOMETHING OUT THERE... SOMETHING DANGEROUS...
AND I SUSPECT IT MEANS TO EAT US...

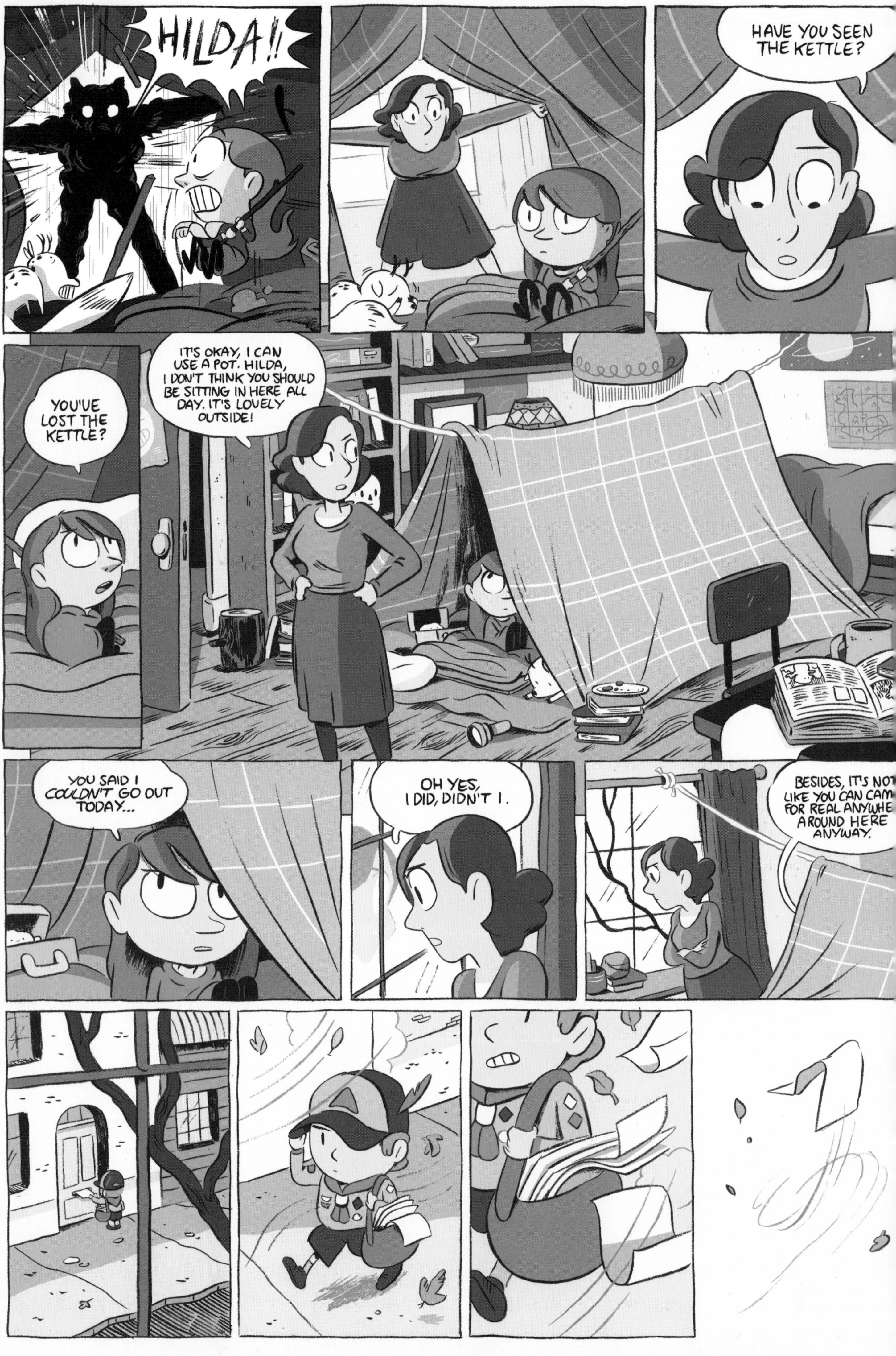
HILDA!!
HAVE YOU SEEN THE KETTLE?
YOU'VE LOST THE KETTLE?
IT'S OKAY, I CAN USE A POT. HILDA, I DON'T THINK YOU SHOULD BE SITTING IN HERE ALL DAY. IT'S LOVELY OUTSIDE!
YOU SAID I COULDN'T GO OUT TODAY...
OH YES, I DID, DIDN'T I.
BESIDES, IT'S NOT LIKE YOU CAN CAM FOR REAL ANYWHE AROUND HERE ANYWAY.

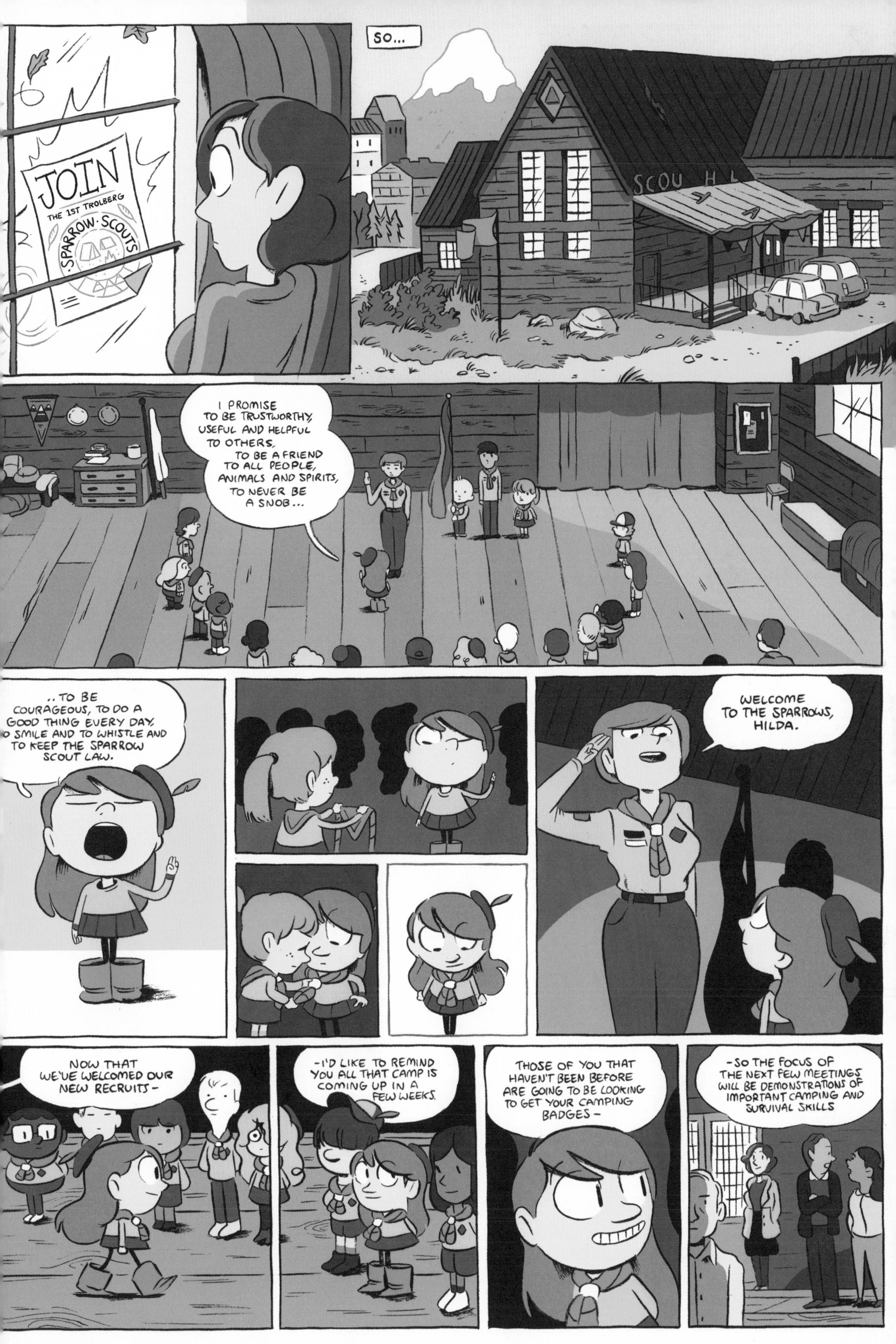
JOIN
THE 1ST TROLBERG
SPARROW · SCOUTS
SO...
SCOU H
I PROMISE TO BE TRUSTWORTHY, USEFUL AND HELPFUL TO OTHERS, TO BE A FRIEND TO ALL PEOPLE, ANIMALS AND SPIRITS, TO NEVER BE A SNOB...
..TO BE COURAGEOUS, TO DO A GOOD THING EVERY DAY, O SMILE AND TO WHISTLE AND TO KEEP THE SPARROW SCOUT LAW.
WELCOME TO THE SPARROWS, HILDA.
NOW THAT WE'VE WELCOMED OUR NEW RECRUITS—
—I'D LIKE TO REMIND YOU ALL THAT CAMP IS COMING UP IN A FEW WEEKS.
THOSE OF YOU THAT HAVEN'T BEEN BEFORE ARE GOING TO BE LOOKING TO GET YOUR CAMPING BADGES—
—SO THE FOCUS OF THE NEXT FEW MEETINGS WILL BE DEMONSTRATIONS OF IMPORTANT CAMPING AND SURVIVAL SKILLS

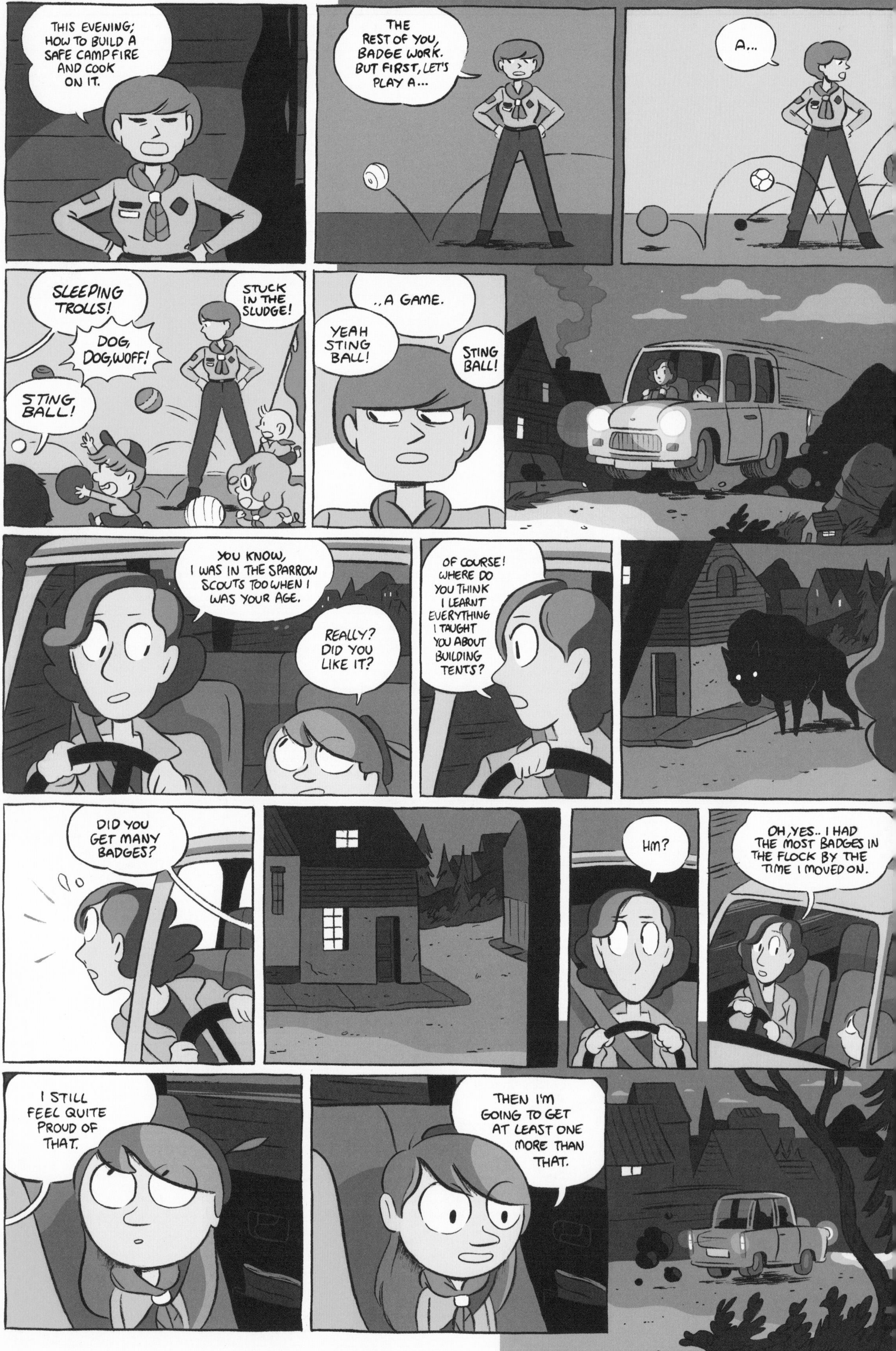
THIS EVENING; HOW TO BUILD A SAFE CAMP FIRE AND COOK ON IT.
THE REST OF YOU, BADGE WORK. BUT FIRST, LET'S PLAY A...
A...
SLEEPING TROLLS!
STUCK IN THE SLUDGE!
DOG, DOG, WOFF!
STING BALL!
.. A GAME.
YEAH STING BALL!
STING BALL!
YOU KNOW, I WAS IN THE SPARROW SCOUTS TOO WHEN I WAS YOUR AGE.
REALLY? DID YOU LIKE IT?
OF COURSE! WHERE DO YOU THINK I LEARNT EVERYTHING I TAUGHT YOU ABOUT BUILDING TENTS?
DID YOU GET MANY BADGES?
HM?
OH, YES.. I HAD THE MOST BADGES IN THE FLOCK BY THE TIME I MOVED ON.
I STILL FEEL QUITE PROUD OF THAT.
THEN I'M GOING TO GET AT LEAST ONE MORE THAN THAT.

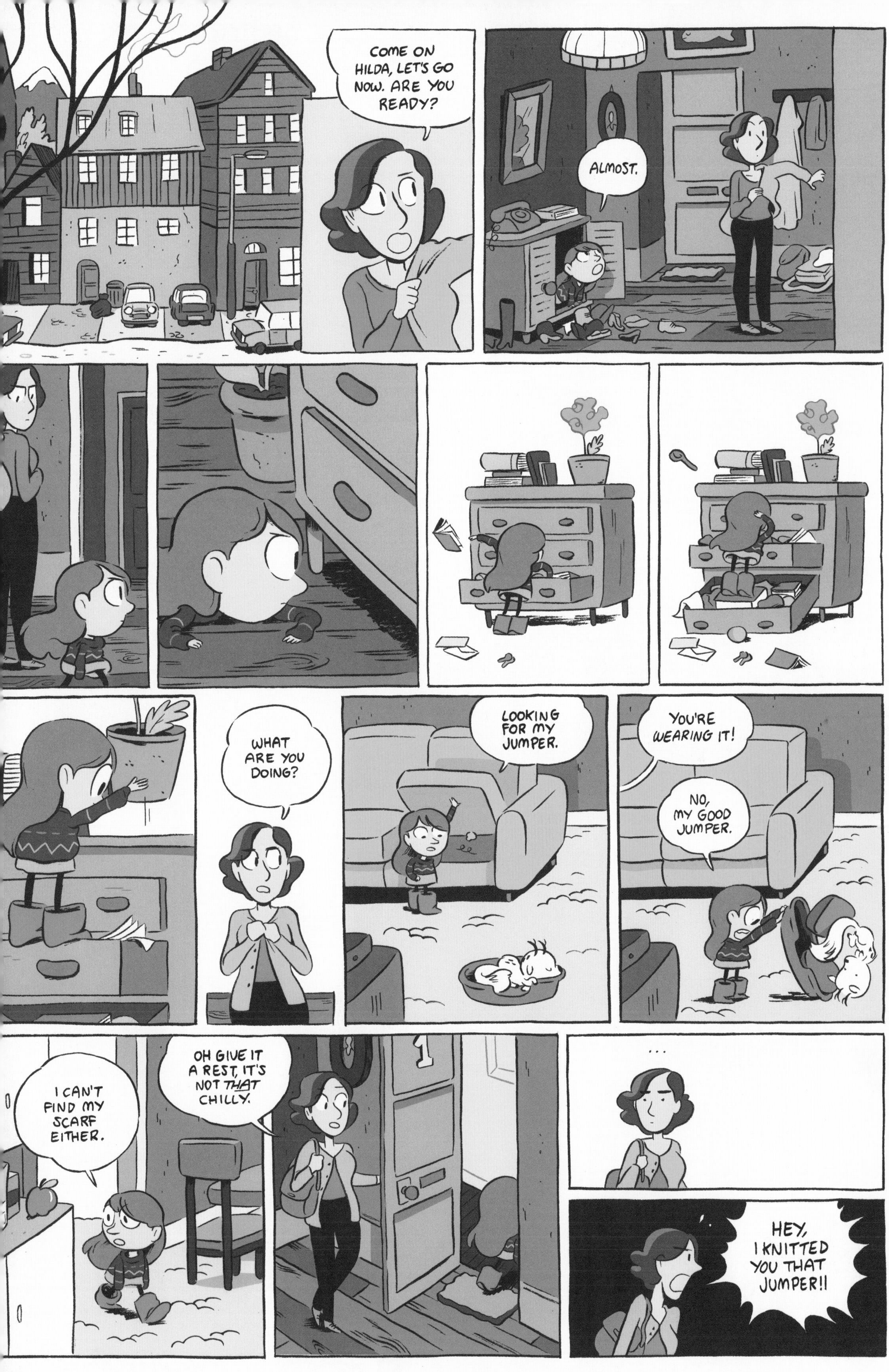
COME ON HILDA, LET'S GO NOW. ARE YOU READY?
ALMOST.
WHAT ARE YOU DOING?
LOOKING FOR MY JUMPER.
YOU'RE WEARING IT!
NO, MY GOOD JUMPER.
I CAN'T FIND MY SCARF EITHER.
OH GIVE IT A REST, IT'S NOT THAT CHILLY.
1
...
HEY, I KNITTED YOU THAT JUMPER!!

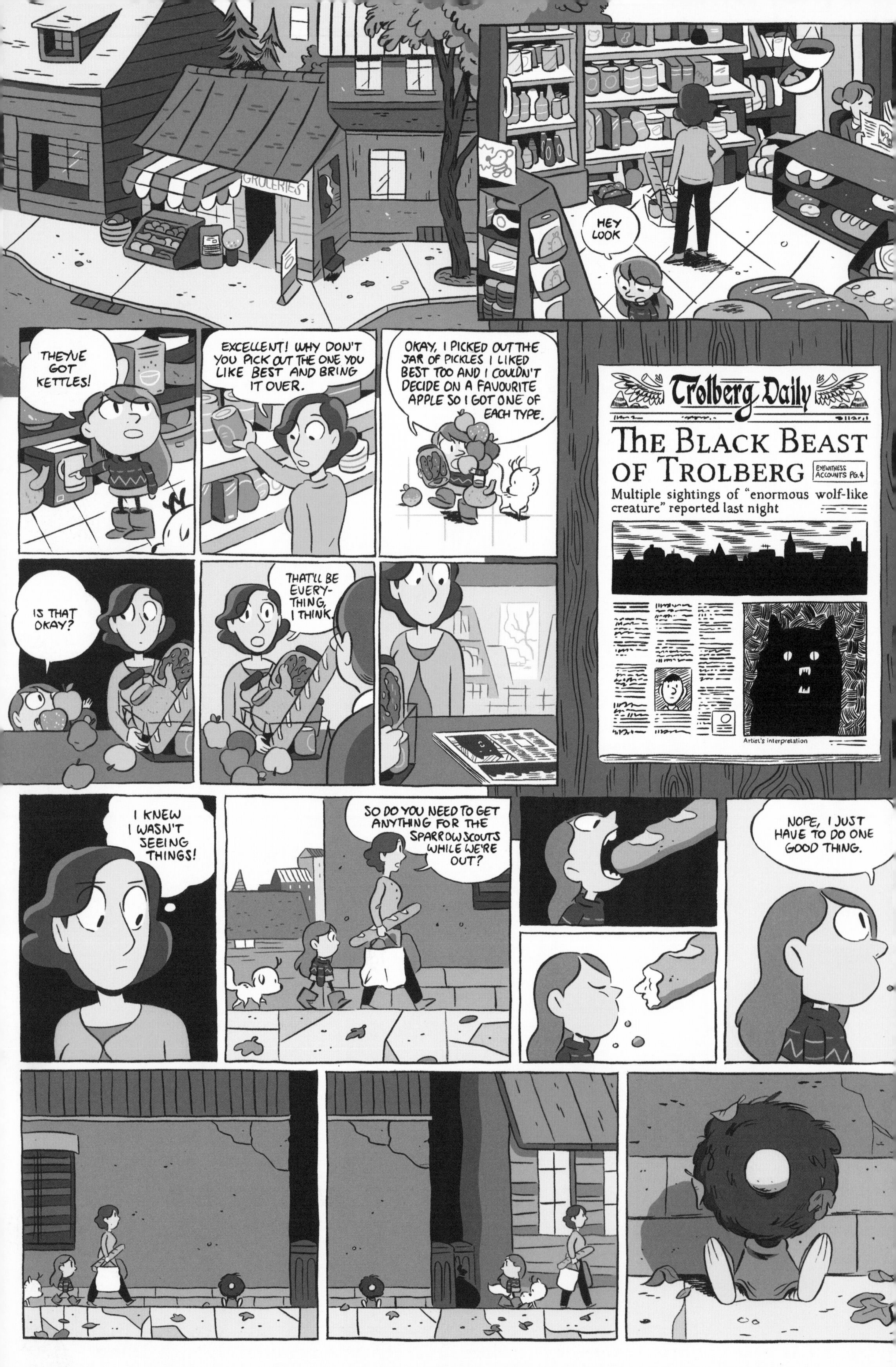
GROCERIES
HEY LOOK
THEY'VE GOT KETTLES!
EXCELLENT! WHY DON'T YOU PICK OUT THE ONE YOU LIKE BEST AND BRING IT OVER.
OKAY, I PICKED OUT THE JAR OF PICKLES I LIKED BEST TOO AND I COULDN'T DECIDE ON A FAVOURITE APPLE SO I GOT ONE OF EACH TYPE.
IS THAT OKAY?
THAT'LL BE EVERY-THING, I THINK.
Trolberg Daily
THE BLACK BEAST OF TROLBERG
EYEWITNESS ACCOUNTS PG.4
Multiple sightings of "enormous wolf-like creature" reported last night
Artist's interpretation
I KNEW I WASN'T SEEING THINGS!
SO DO YOU NEED TO GET ANYTHING FOR THE SPARROW SCOUTS WHILE WE'RE OUT?
NOPE, I JUST HAVE TO DO ONE GOOD THING.

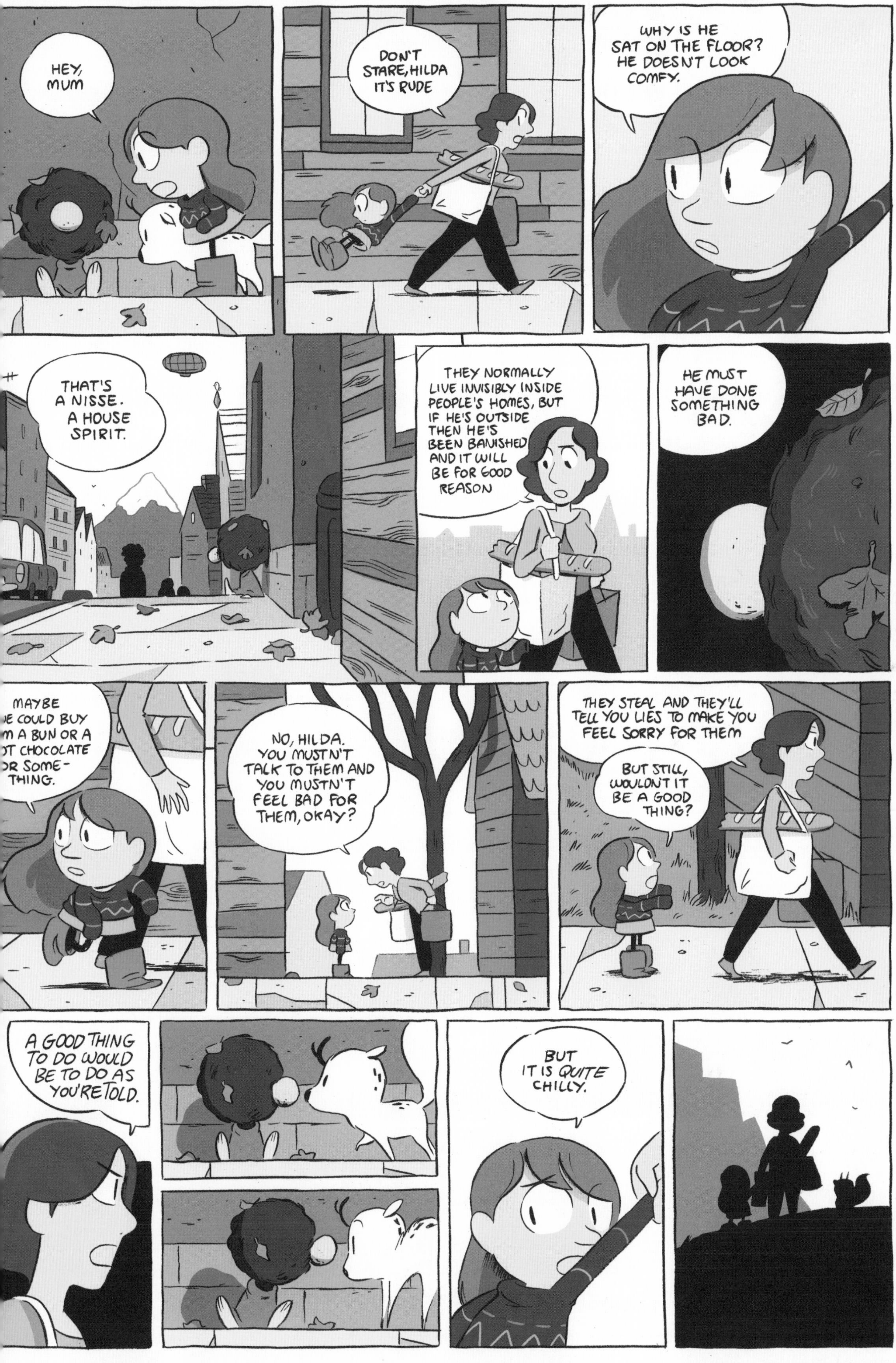
HEY, MUM
DON'T STARE, HILDA IT'S RUDE
WHY IS HE SAT ON THE FLOOR? HE DOESN'T LOOK COMFY.
THAT'S A NISSE. A HOUSE SPIRIT.
THEY NORMALLY LIVE INVISIBLY INSIDE PEOPLE'S HOMES, BUT IF HE'S OUTSIDE THEN HE'S BEEN BANISHED AND IT WILL BE FOR GOOD REASON
HE MUST HAVE DONE SOMETHING BAD.
MAYBE
COULD BUY
A BUN OR A
CHOCOLATE
SOME-
THING.
NO, HILDA. YOU MUSTN'T TALK TO THEM AND YOU MUSTN'T FEEL BAD FOR THEM, OKAY?
THEY STEAL AND THEY'LL TELL YOU LIES TO MAKE YOU FEEL SORRY FOR THEM
BUT STILL, WOULDN'T IT BE A GOOD THING?
A GOOD THING TO DO WOULD BE TO DO AS YOU'RE TOLD.
BUT IT IS QUITE CHILLY.

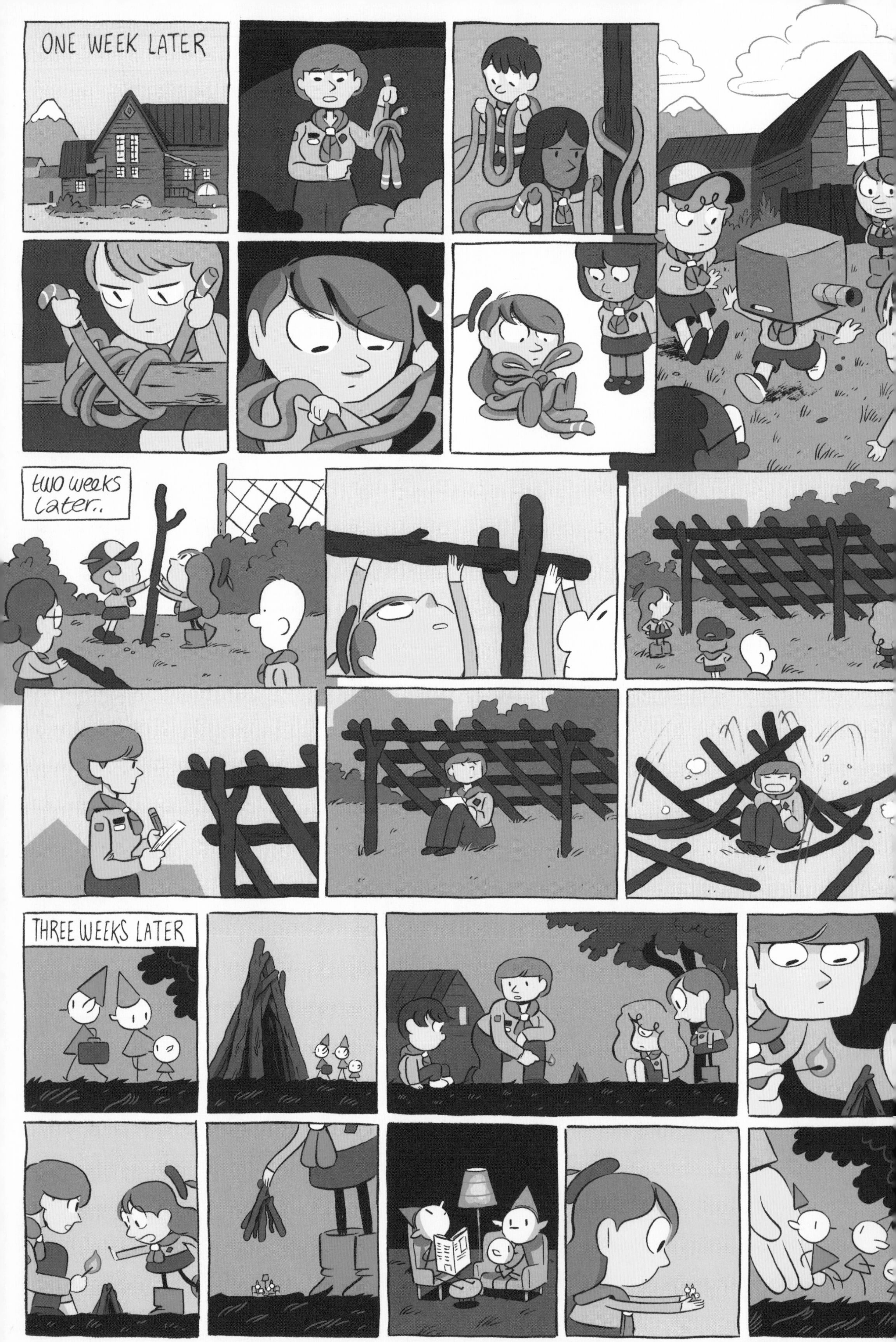
ONE WEEK LATER
two weeks later..
THREE WEEKS LATER

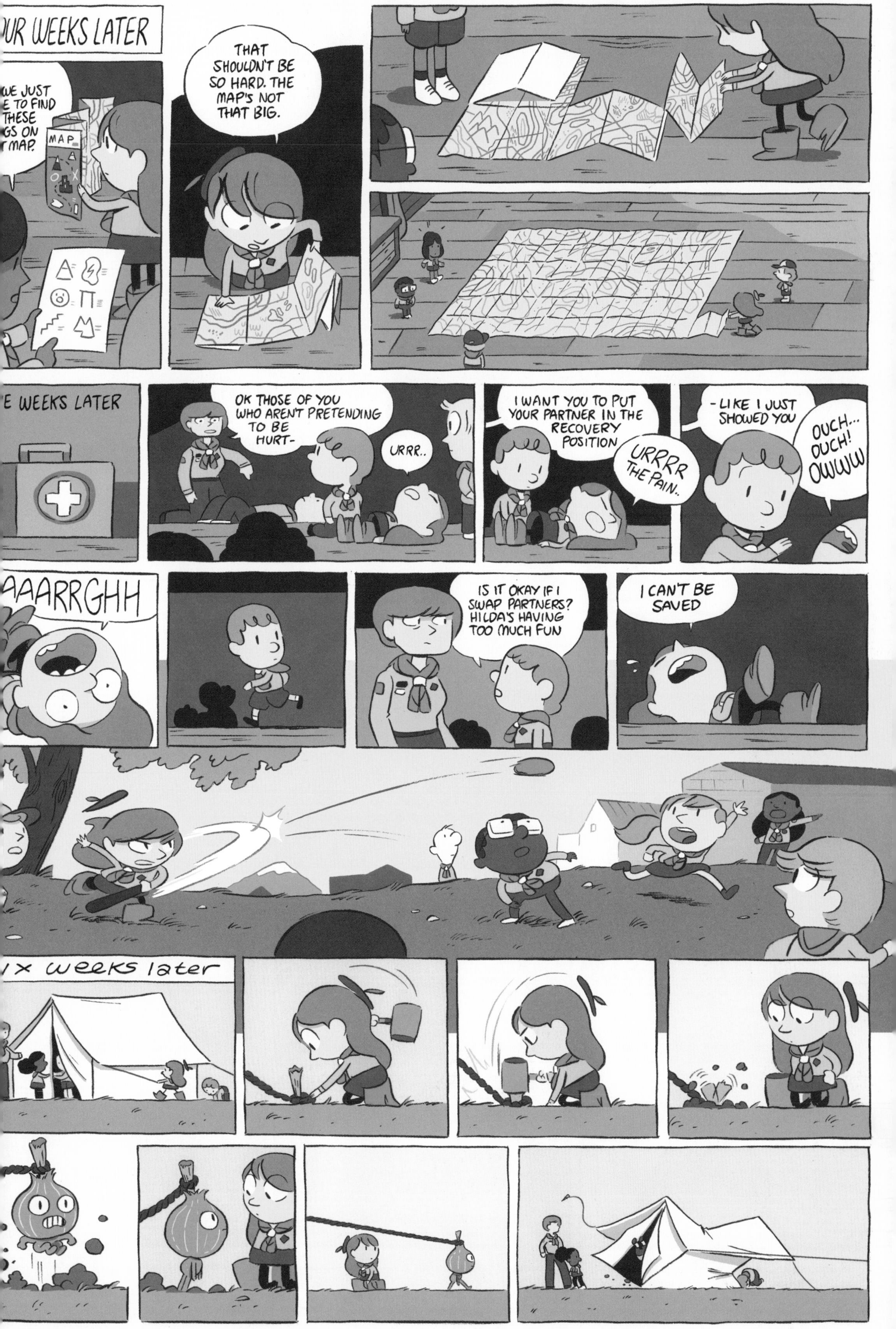

OUR WEEKS LATER
WE JUST
E TO FIND
THESE
GS ON
T MAP.
MAP
THAT SHOULDN'T BE SO HARD. THE MAP'S NOT THAT BIG.
E WEEKS LATER
OK THOSE OF YOU WHO AREN'T PRETENDING TO BE HURT-
URRR..
I WANT YOU TO PUT YOUR PARTNER IN THE RECOVERY POSITION
URRRR THE PAIN..
-LIKE I JUST SHOWED YOU
OUCH... OUCH! OWWW
AAARRGHH
IS IT OKAY IF I SWAP PARTNERS? HILDA'S HAVING TOO MUCH FUN
I CAN'T BE SAVED
IX WEEKS LATER

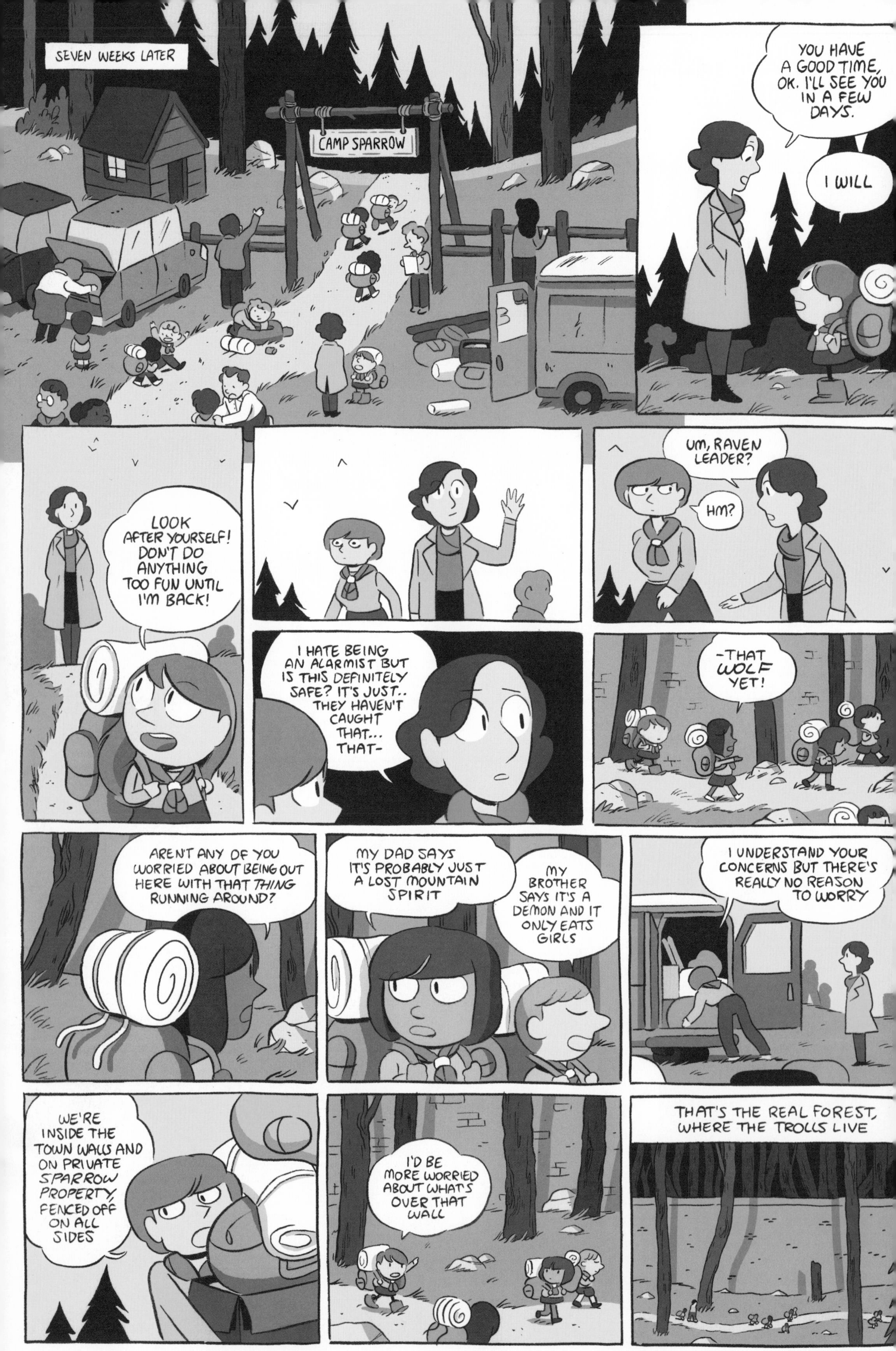
SEVEN WEEKS LATER
CAMP SPARROW
3
YOU HAVE A GOOD TIME, OK. I'LL SEE YOU IN A FEW DAYS.
I WILL
LOOK AFTER YOURSELF! DON'T DO ANYTHING TOO FUN UNTIL I'M BACK!
UM, RAVEN LEADER?
HM?
I HATE BEING AN ALARMIST BUT IS THIS DEFINITELY SAFE? IT'S JUST.. THEY HAVEN'T CAUGHT THAT... THAT-
-THAT WOLF YET!
AREN'T ANY OF YOU WORRIED ABOUT BEING OUT HERE WITH THAT THING RUNNING AROUND?
MY DAD SAYS IT'S PROBABLY JUST A LOST MOUNTAIN SPIRIT
MY BROTHER SAYS IT'S A DEMON AND IT ONLY EATS GIRLS
I UNDERSTAND YOUR CONCERNS BUT THERE'S REALLY NO REASON TO WORRY
WE'RE INSIDE THE TOWN WALLS AND ON PRIVATE SPARROW PROPERTY, FENCED OFF ON ALL SIDES
I'D BE MORE WORRIED ABOUT WHAT'S OVER THAT WALL
THAT'S THE REAL FOREST, WHERE THE TROLLS LIVE

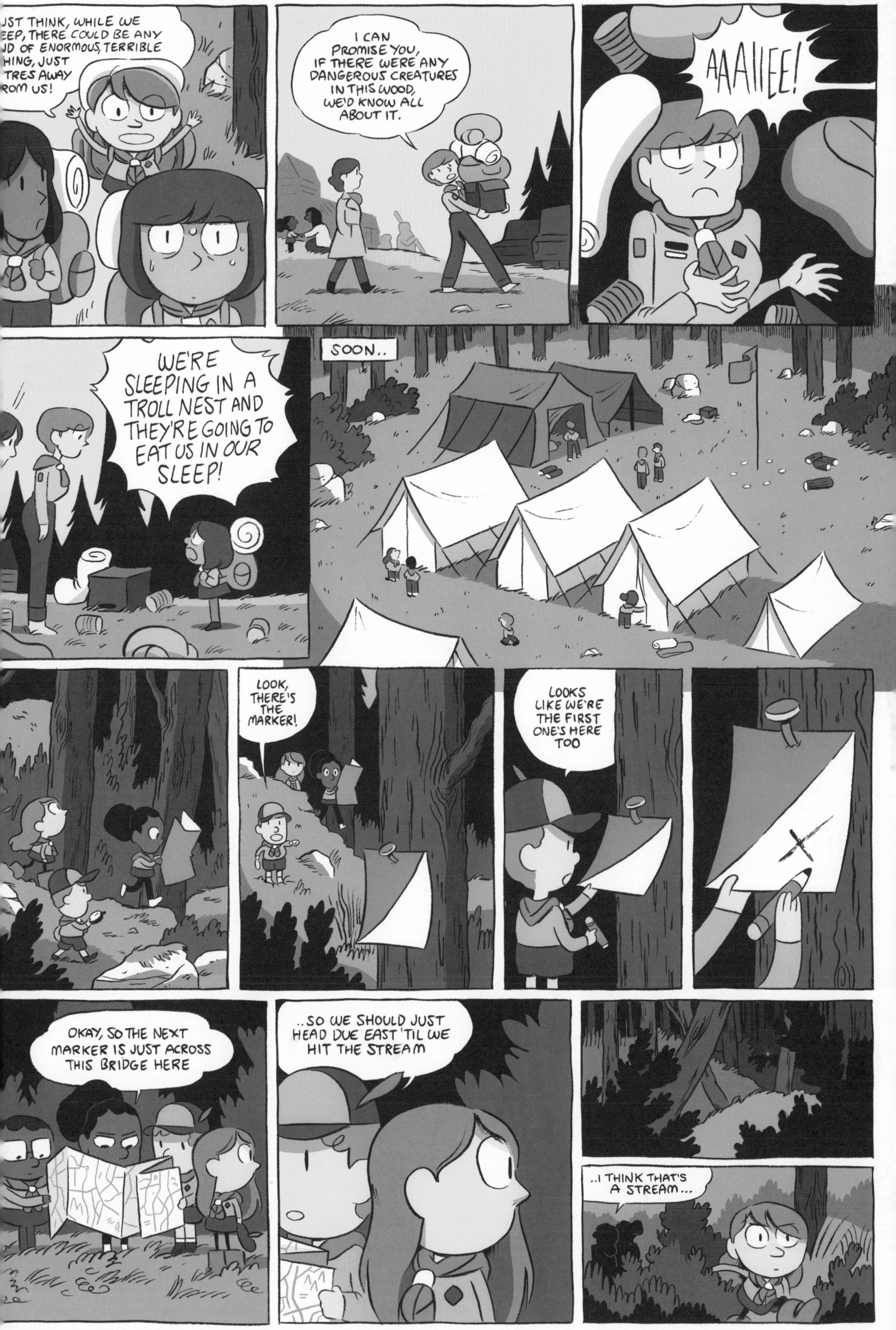
UST THINK, WHILE WE
EEP, THERE COULD BE ANY
ND OF ENORMOUS, TERRIBLE
HING, JUST
TRES AWAY
ROM US!
I CAN PROMISE YOU, IF THERE WERE ANY DANGEROUS CREATURES IN THIS WOOD, WE'D KNOW ALL ABOUT IT.
AAAIIEE!
WE'RE SLEEPING IN A TROLL NEST AND THEY'RE GOING TO EAT US IN OUR SLEEP!
SOON..
LOOK, THERE'S THE MARKER!
LOOKS LIKE WE'RE THE FIRST ONE'S HERE TOO
OKAY, SO THE NEXT MARKER IS JUST ACROSS THIS BRIDGE HERE
..SO WE SHOULD JUST HEAD DUE EAST 'TIL WE HIT THE STREAM
..I THINK THAT'S A STREAM...

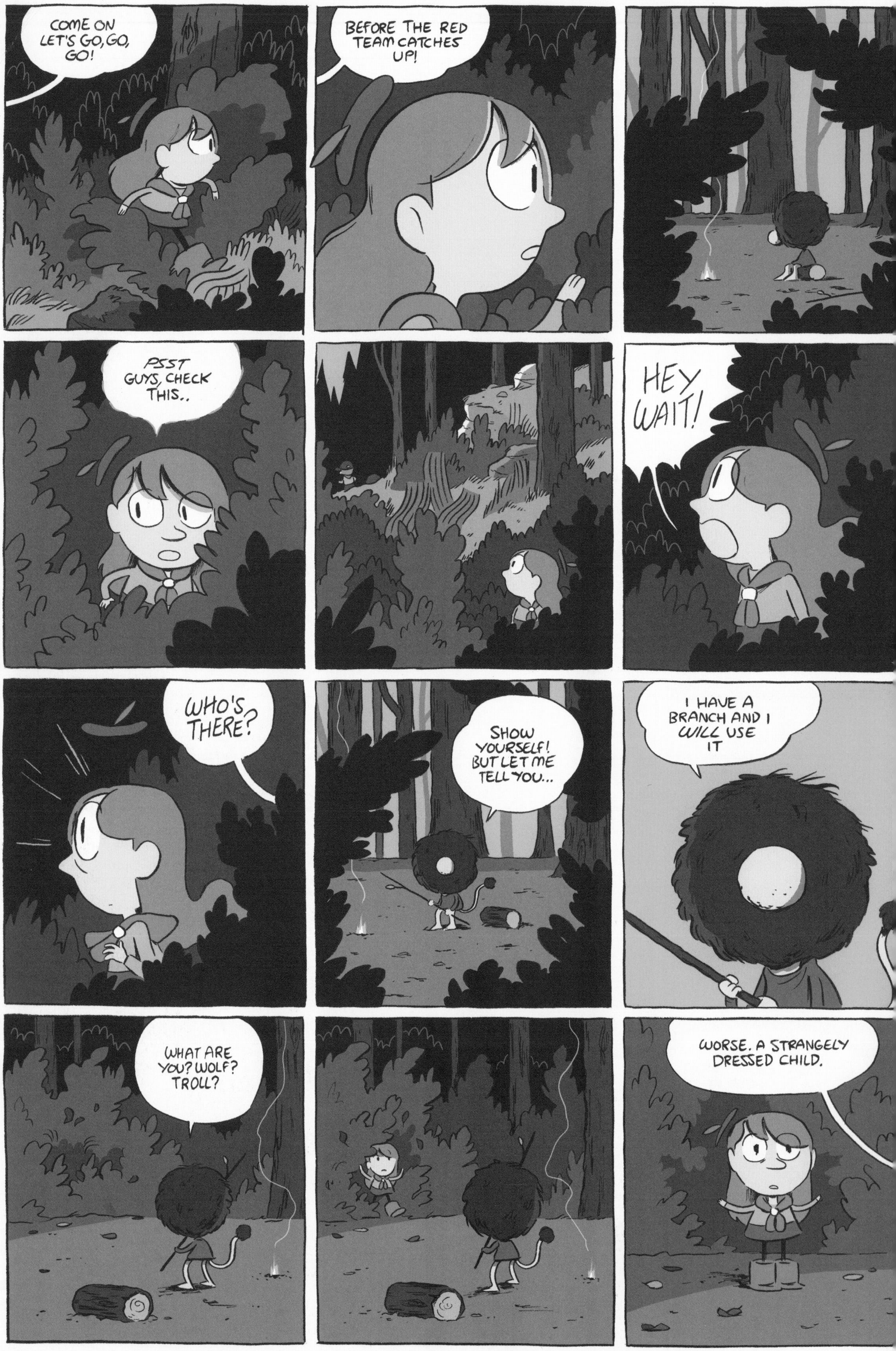
COME ON LET'S GO, GO, GO!
BEFORE THE RED TEAM CATCHES UP!
PSST GUYS, CHECK THIS..
HEY WAIT!
WHO'S THERE?
SHOW YOURSELF! BUT LET ME TELL YOU...
I HAVE A BRANCH AND I WILL USE IT
WHAT ARE YOU? WOLF? TROLL?
WORSE. A STRANGELY DRESSED CHILD.

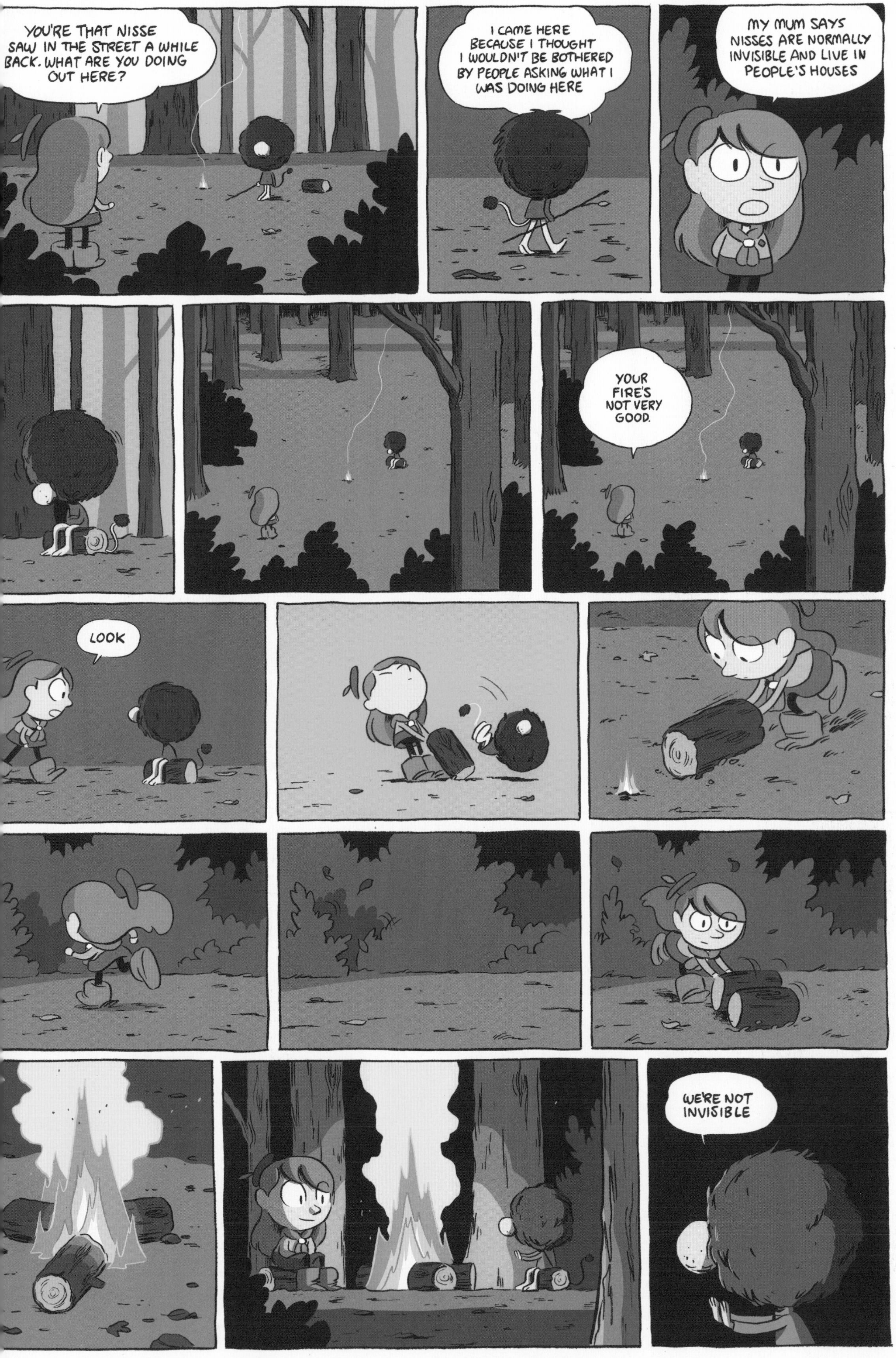
YOU'RE THAT NISSE SAW IN THE STREET A WHILE BACK. WHAT ARE YOU DOING OUT HERE?
I CAME HERE BECAUSE I THOUGHT I WOULDN'T BE BOTHERED BY PEOPLE ASKING WHAT I WAS DOING HERE
MY MUM SAYS NISSES ARE NORMALLY INVISIBLE AND LIVE IN PEOPLE'S HOUSES
YOUR FIRE'S NOT VERY GOOD.
LOOK
WE'RE NOT INVISIBLE

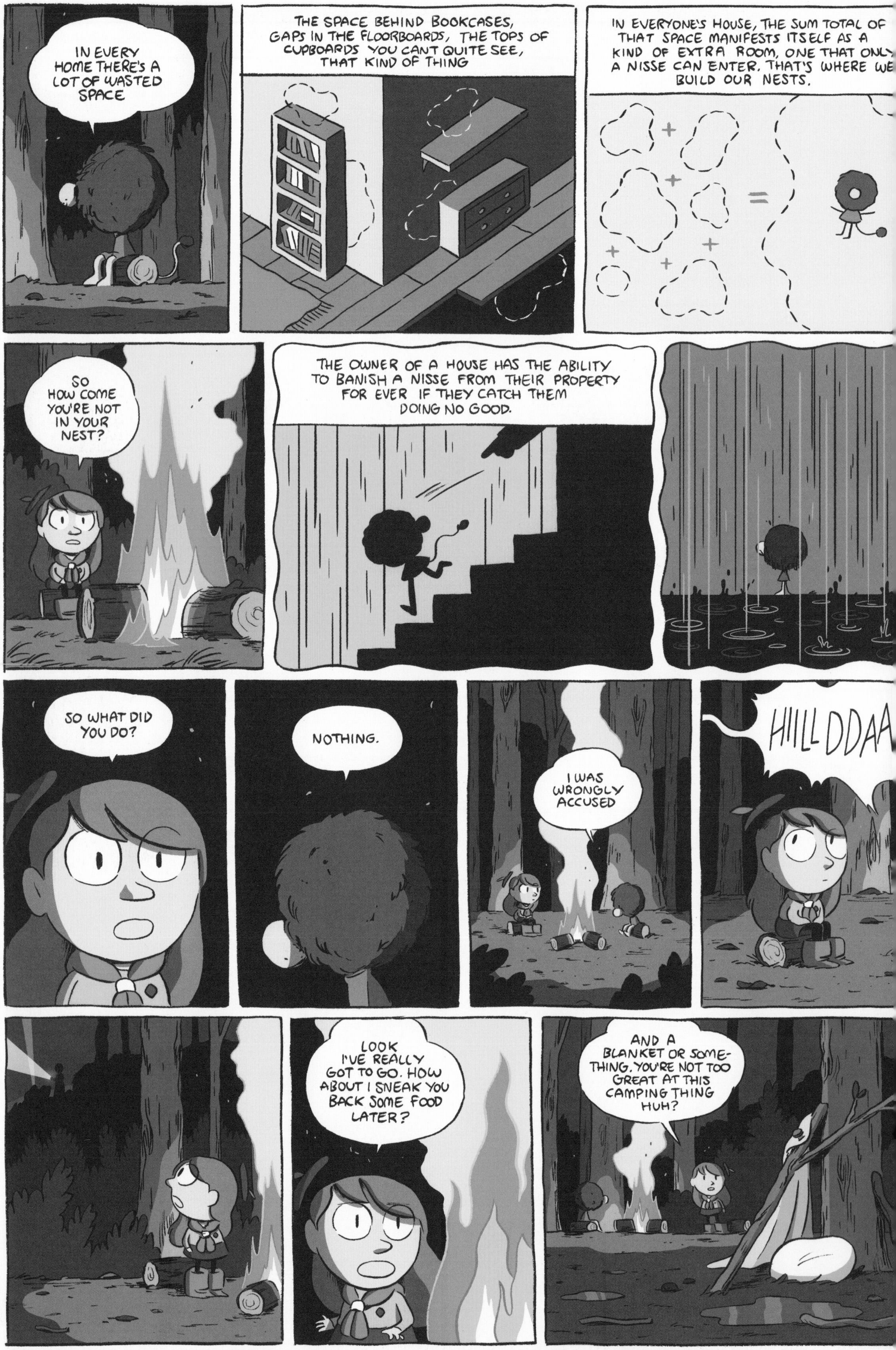
IN EVERY HOME THERE'S A LOT OF WASTED SPACE
THE SPACE BEHIND BOOKCASES, GAPS IN THE FLOORBOARDS, THE TOPS OF CUPBOARDS YOU CANT QUITE SEE, THAT KIND OF THING
IN EVERYONE'S HOUSE, THE SUM TOTAL OF THAT SPACE MANIFESTS ITSELF AS A KIND OF EXTRA ROOM, ONE THAT ONLY A NISSE CAN ENTER. THAT'S WHERE WE BUILD OUR NESTS.
+
=
SO HOW COME YOU'RE NOT IN YOUR NEST?
THE OWNER OF A HOUSE HAS THE ABILITY TO BANISH A NISSE FROM THEIR PROPERTY FOR EVER IF THEY CATCH THEM DOING NO GOOD.
SO WHAT DID YOU DO?
NOTHING.
I WAS WRONGLY ACCUSED
HILLDDAA
LOOK I'VE REALLY GOT TO GO. HOW ABOUT I SNEAK YOU BACK SOME FOOD LATER?
AND A BLANKET OR SOME-THING. YOU'RE NOT TOO GREAT AT THIS CAMPING THING HUH?

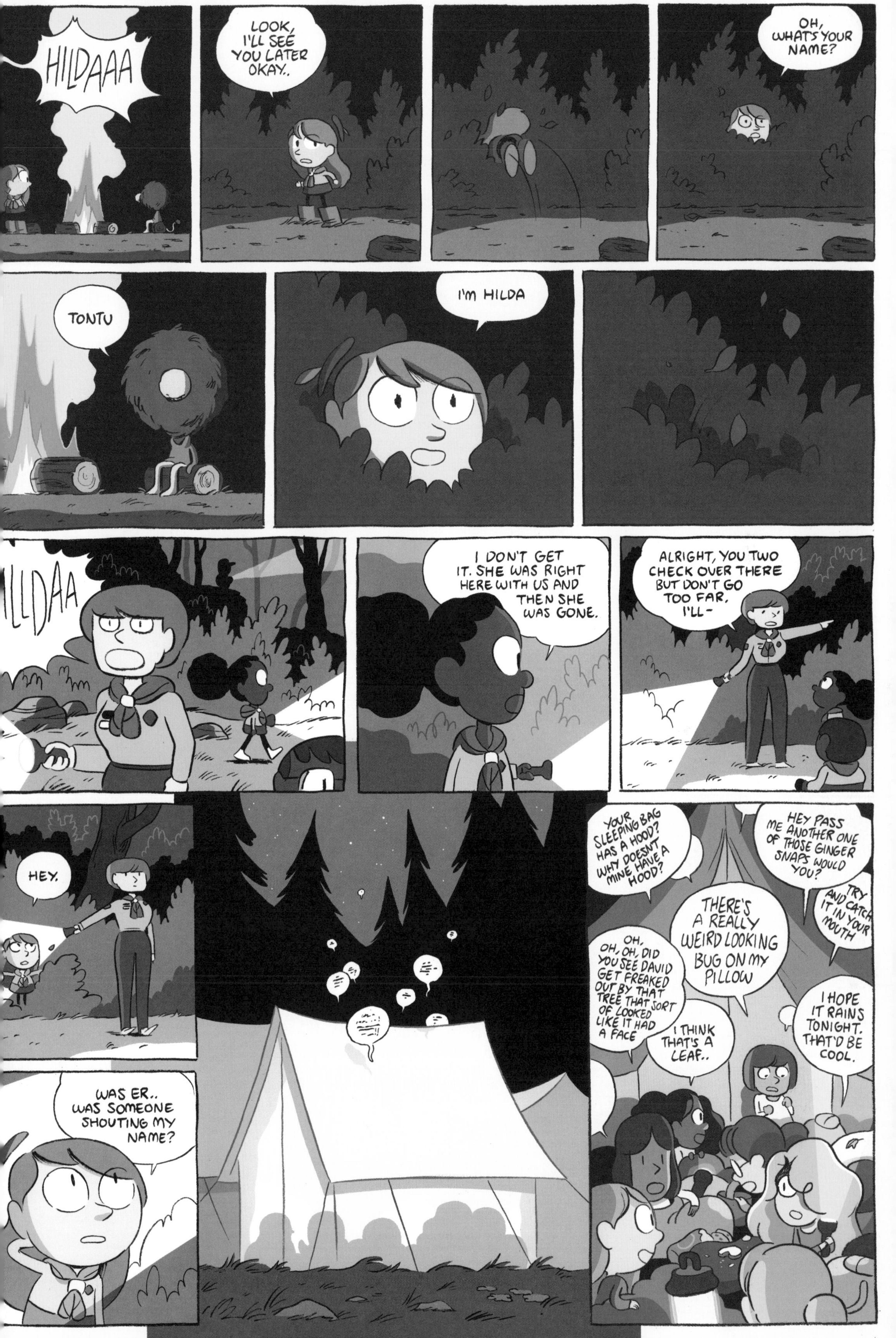
HILDAAA
LOOK, I'LL SEE YOU LATER OKAY..
OH, WHAT'S YOUR NAME?
TONTU
I'M HILDA
HILLDAA
I DON'T GET IT. SHE WAS RIGHT HERE WITH US AND THEN SHE WAS GONE.
ALRIGHT, YOU TWO CHECK OVER THERE BUT DON'T GO TOO FAR, I'LL-
HEY.
WAS ER.. WAS SOMEONE SHOUTING MY NAME?
YOUR SLEEPING BAG HAS A HOOD? WHY DOESN'T MINE HAVE A HOOD?
HEY PASS ME ANOTHER ONE OF THOSE GINGER SNAPS WOULD YOU?
TRY AND CATCH IT IN YOUR MOUTH
THERE'S A REALLY WEIRD LOOKING BUG ON MY PILLOW
OH, OH, OH, DID YOU SEE DAVID GET FREAKED OUT BY THAT TREE THAT SORT OF LOOKED LIKE IT HAD A FACE
I THINK THAT'S A LEAF..
I HOPE IT RAINS TONIGHT. THAT'D BE COOL.

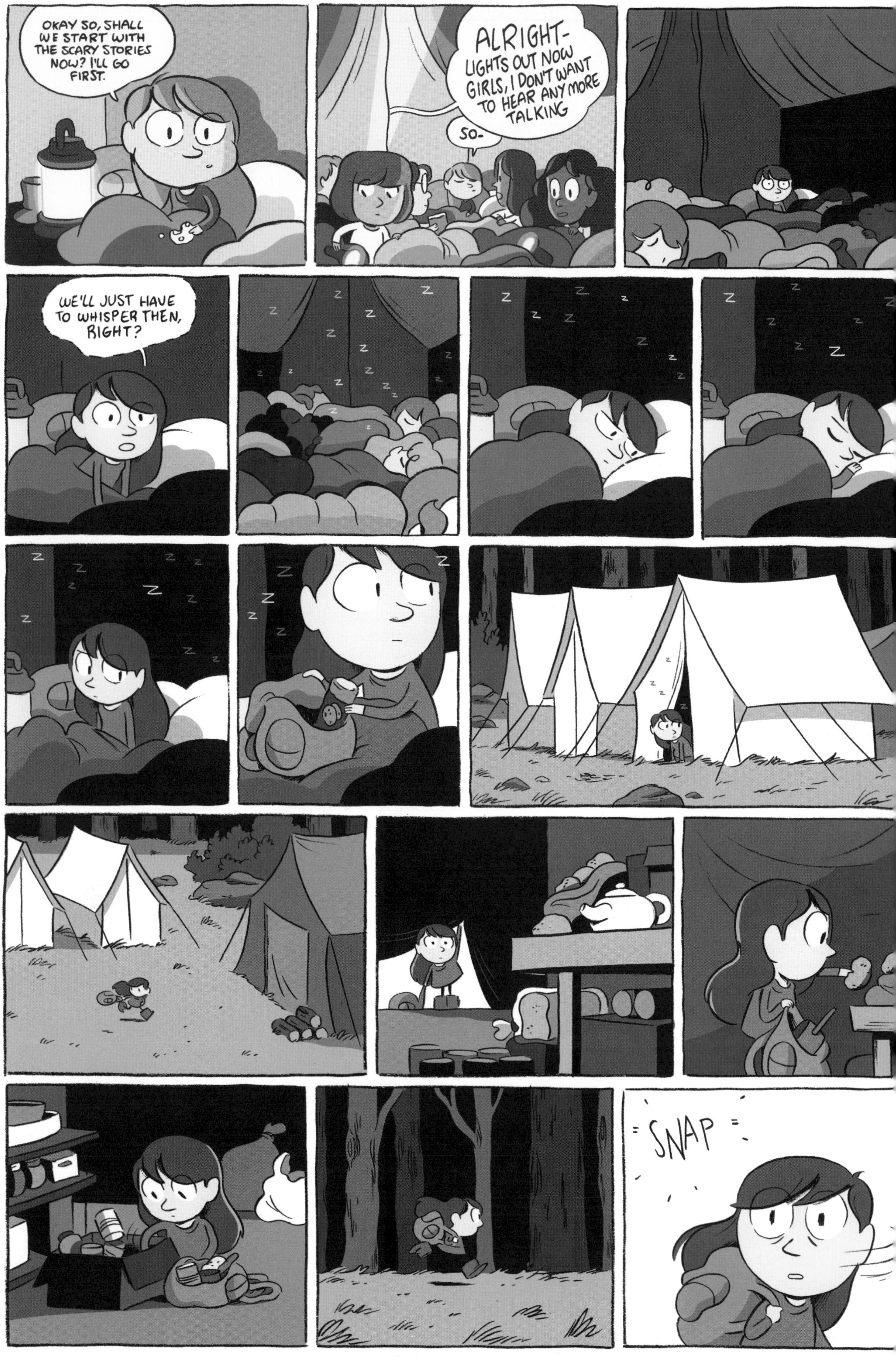

OKAY SO, SHALL WE START WITH THE SCARY STORIES NOW? I'LL GO FIRST.
ALRIGHT- LIGHTS OUT NOW GIRLS, I DON'T WANT TO HEAR ANY MORE TALKING
SO-
WE'LL JUST HAVE TO WHISPER THEN, RIGHT?
SNAP

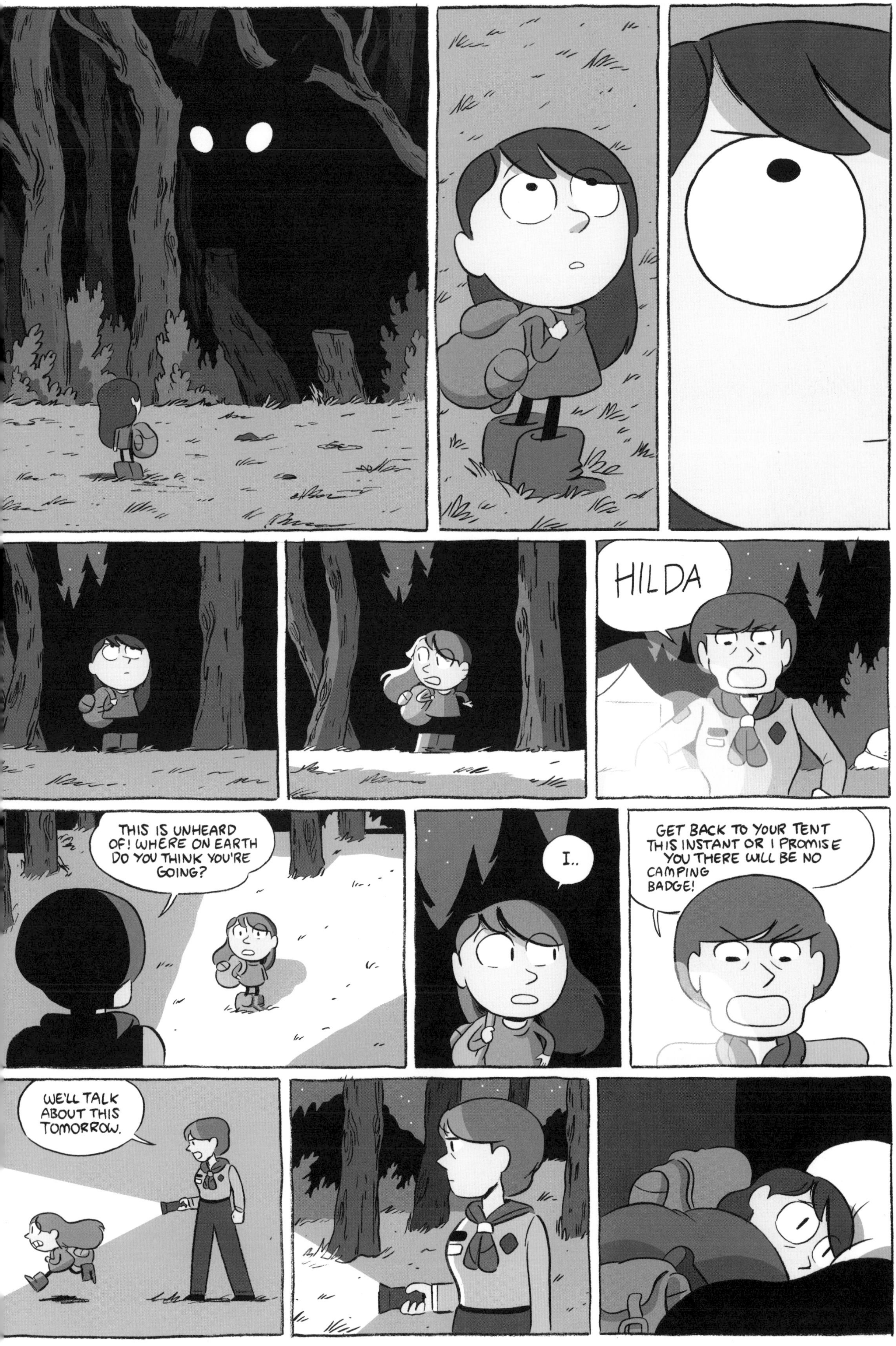
HILDA
THIS IS UNHEARD OF! WHERE ON EARTH DO YOU THINK YOU'RE GOING?
I..
GET BACK TO YOUR TENT THIS INSTANT OR I PROMISE YOU THERE WILL BE NO CAMPING BADGE!
WE'LL TALK ABOUT THIS TOMORROW.

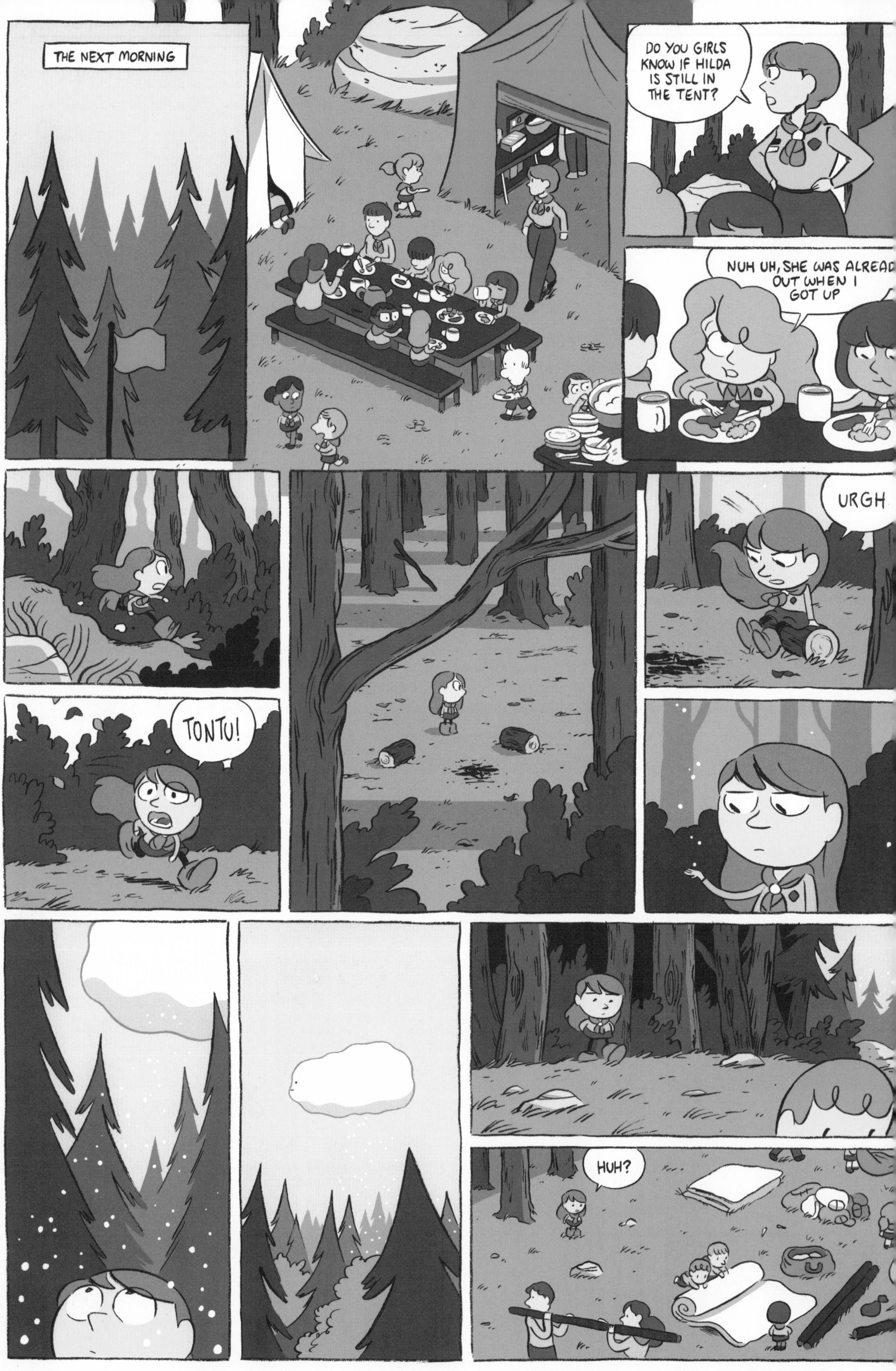
THE NEXT MORNING
DO YOU GIRLS KNOW IF HILDA IS STILL IN THE TENT?
NUH UH, SHE WAS ALREAD OUT WHEN I GOT UP
TONTU!
URGH
HUH?

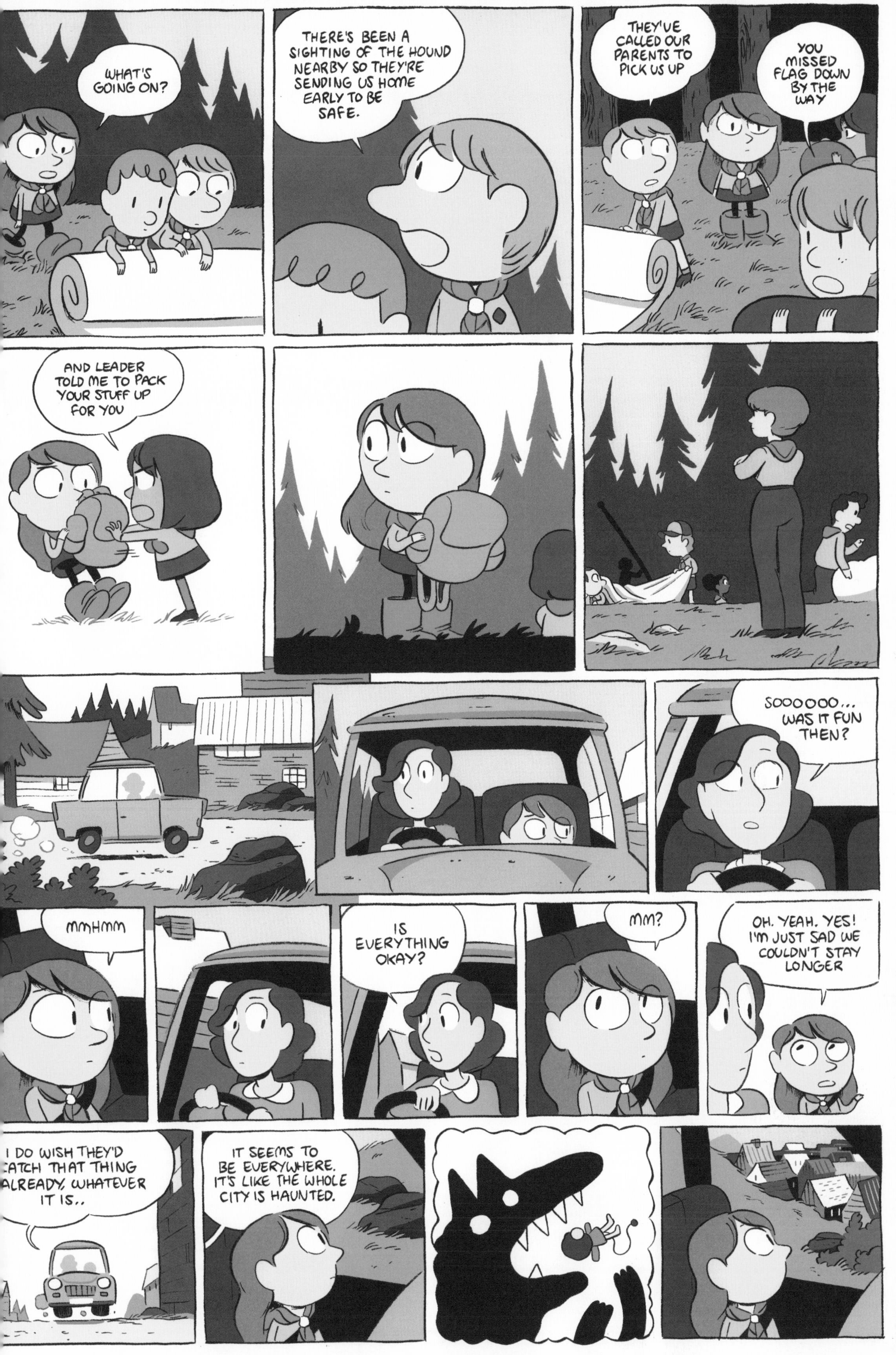
WHAT'S GOING ON?
THERE'S BEEN A SIGHTING OF THE HOUND NEARBY SO THEY'RE SENDING US HOME EARLY TO BE SAFE.
THEY'VE CALLED OUR PARENTS TO PICK US UP
YOU MISSED FLAG DOWN BY THE WAY
AND LEADER TOLD ME TO PACK YOUR STUFF UP FOR YOU
SOOOOOO... WAS IT FUN THEN?
MMHMM
IS EVERYTHING OKAY?
MM?
OH. YEAH. YES! I'M JUST SAD WE COULDN'T STAY LONGER
I DO WISH THEY'D CATCH THAT THING ALREADY, WHATEVER IT IS..
IT SEEMS TO BE EVERYWHERE. IT'S LIKE THE WHOLE CITY IS HAUNTED.

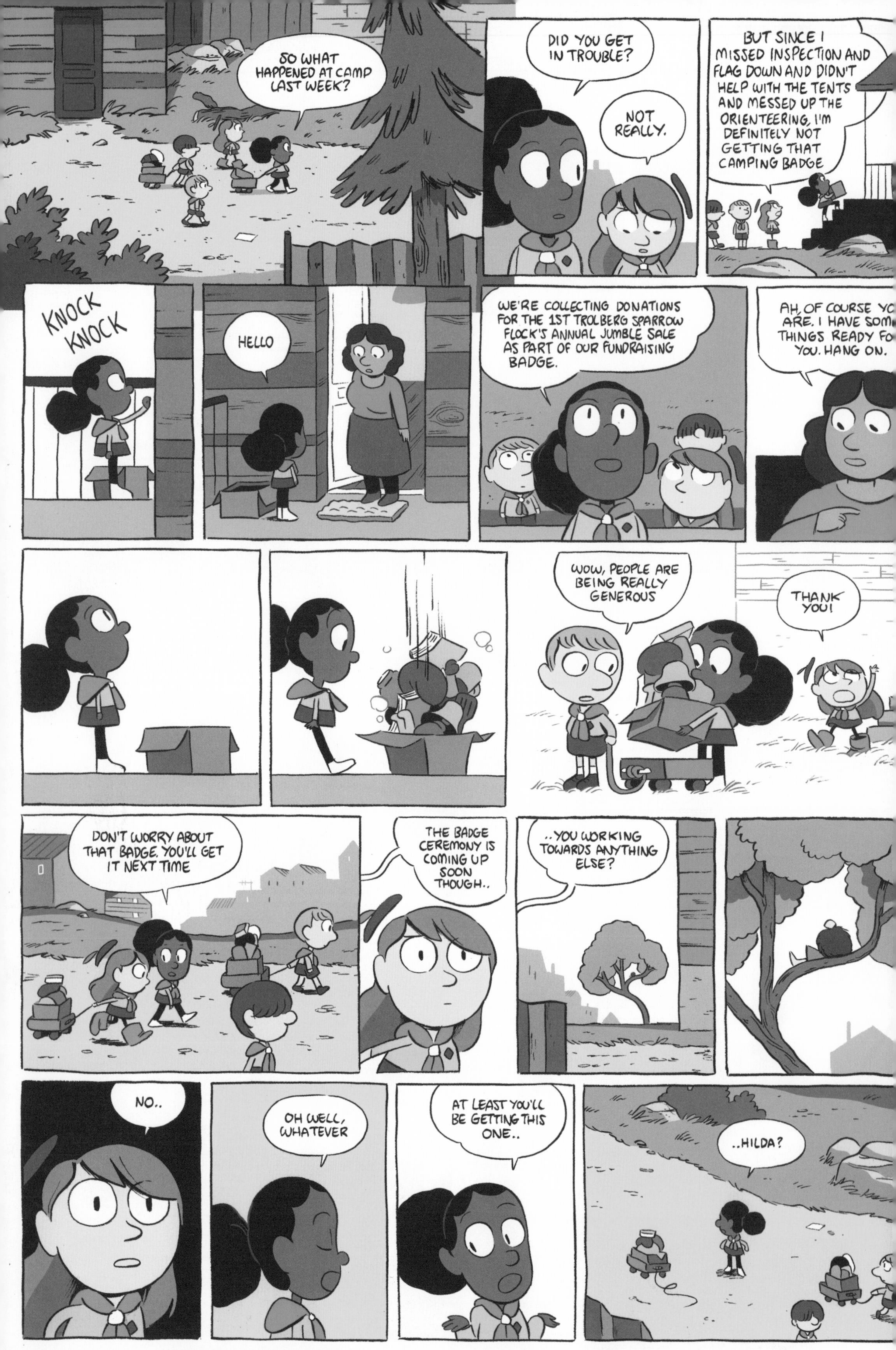
SO WHAT HAPPENED AT CAMP LAST WEEK?
DID YOU GET IN TROUBLE?
NOT REALLY.
BUT SINCE I MISSED INSPECTION AND FLAG DOWN AND DIDN'T HELP WITH THE TENTS AND MESSED UP THE ORIENTEERING, I'M DEFINITELY NOT GETTING THAT CAMPING BADGE
KNOCK KNOCK
HELLO
WE'RE COLLECTING DONATIONS FOR THE 1ST TROLBERG SPARROW FLOCK'S ANNUAL JUMBLE SALE AS PART OF OUR FUNDRAISING BADGE.
AH, OF COURSE YO ARE. I HAVE SOM THINGS READY FO YOU. HANG ON.
WOW, PEOPLE ARE BEING REALLY GENEROUS
THANK YOU!
DON'T WORRY ABOUT THAT BADGE. YOU'LL GET IT NEXT TIME
THE BADGE CEREMONY IS COMING UP SOON THOUGH..
..YOU WORKING TOWARDS ANYTHING ELSE?
NO..
OH WELL, WHATEVER
AT LEAST YOU'LL BE GETTING THIS ONE..
..HILDA?

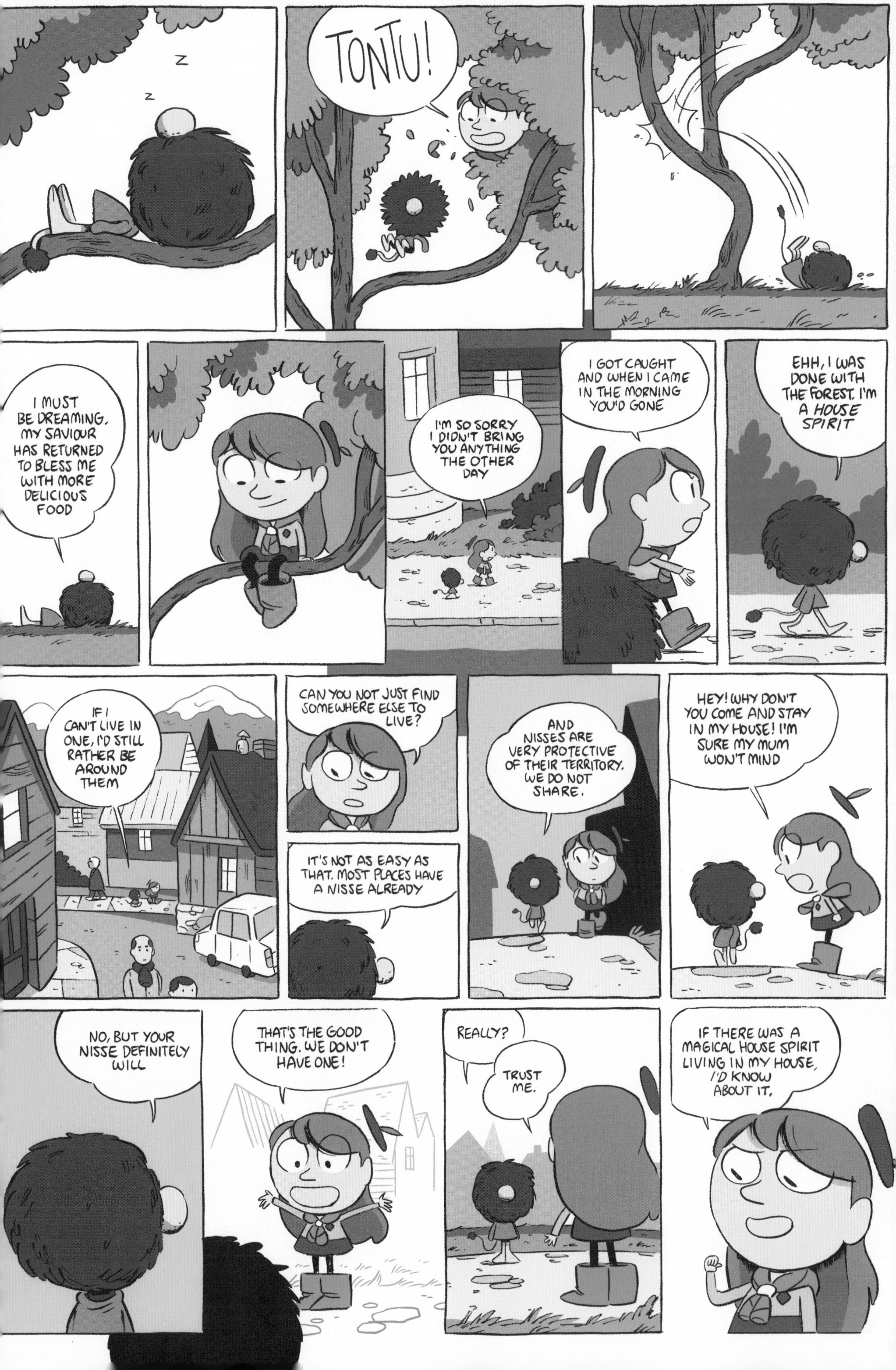
Z
Z
TONTU!
I MUST BE DREAMING. MY SAVIOUR HAS RETURNED TO BLESS ME WITH MORE DELICIOUS FOOD
I'M SO SORRY I DIDN'T BRING YOU ANYTHING THE OTHER DAY
I GOT CAUGHT AND WHEN I CAME IN THE MORNING YOU'D GONE
EHH, I WAS DONE WITH THE FOREST. I'M A HOUSE SPIRIT
IF I CAN'T LIVE IN ONE, I'D STILL RATHER BE AROUND THEM
CAN YOU NOT JUST FIND SOMEWHERE ELSE TO LIVE?
IT'S NOT AS EASY AS THAT. MOST PLACES HAVE A NISSE ALREADY
AND NISSES ARE VERY PROTECTIVE OF THEIR TERRITORY. WE DO NOT SHARE.
HEY! WHY DON'T YOU COME AND STAY IN MY HOUSE! I'M SURE MY MUM WON'T MIND
NO, BUT YOUR NISSE DEFINITELY WILL
THAT'S THE GOOD THING. WE DON'T HAVE ONE!
REALLY?
TRUST ME.
IF THERE WAS A MAGICAL HOUSE SPIRIT LIVING IN MY HOUSE, I'D KNOW ABOUT IT.

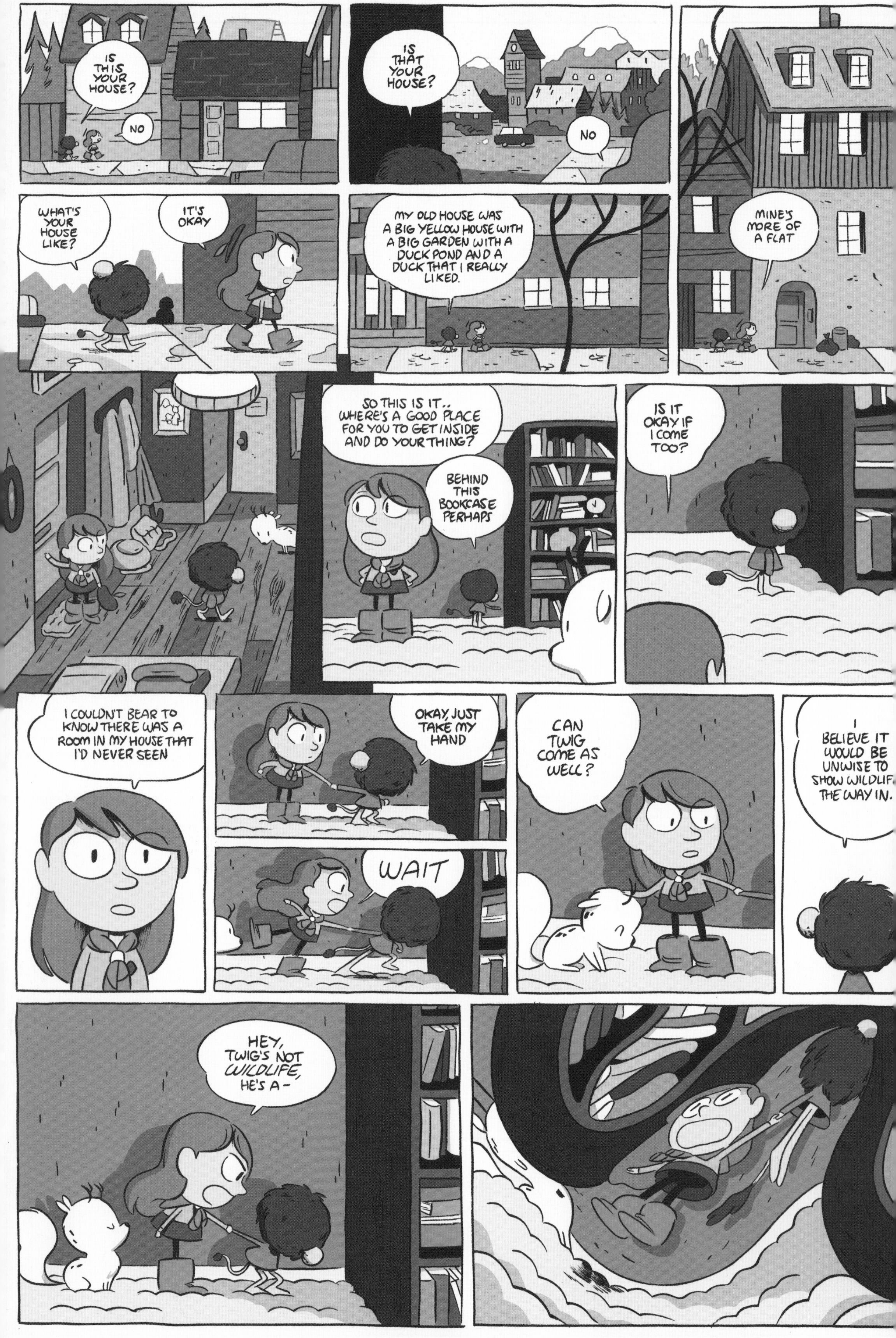
IS THIS YOUR HOUSE?
NO
IS THAT YOUR HOUSE?
NO
WHAT'S YOUR HOUSE LIKE?
IT'S OKAY
MY OLD HOUSE WAS A BIG YELLOW HOUSE WITH A BIG GARDEN WITH A DUCK POND AND A DUCK THAT I REALLY LIKED.
MINE'S MORE OF A FLAT
SO THIS IS IT.. WHERE'S A GOOD PLACE FOR YOU TO GET INSIDE AND DO YOUR THING?
BEHIND THIS BOOKCASE PERHAPS
IS IT OKAY IF I COME TOO?
I COULDN'T BEAR TO KNOW THERE WAS A ROOM IN MY HOUSE THAT I'D NEVER SEEN
OKAY, JUST TAKE MY HAND
WAIT
CAN TWIG COME AS WELL?
I BELIEVE IT WOULD BE UNWISE TO SHOW WILDLIF. THE WAY IN.
HEY, TWIG'S NOT *WILDLIFE*, HE'S A -

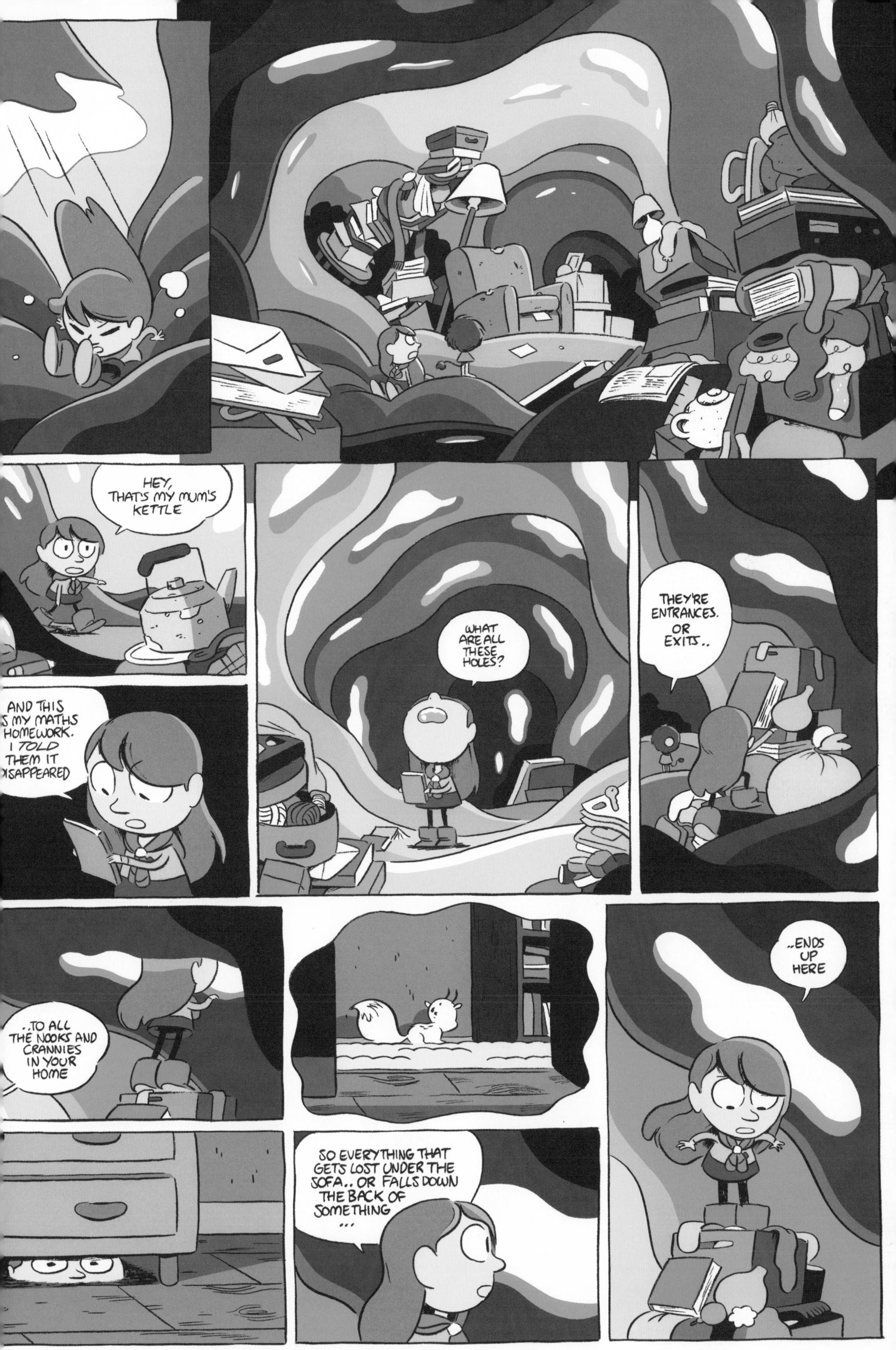

HEY, THAT'S MY MUM'S KETTLE
AND THIS S MY MATHS HOMEWORK. I TOLD THEM IT SAPPEARED
WHAT ARE ALL THESE HOLES?
THEY'RE ENTRANCES. OR EXITS..
..TO ALL THE NOOKS AND CRANNIES IN YOUR HOME
SO EVERYTHING THAT GETS LOST UNDER THE SOFA.. OR FALLS DOWN THE BACK OF SOMETHING ...
..ENDS UP HERE

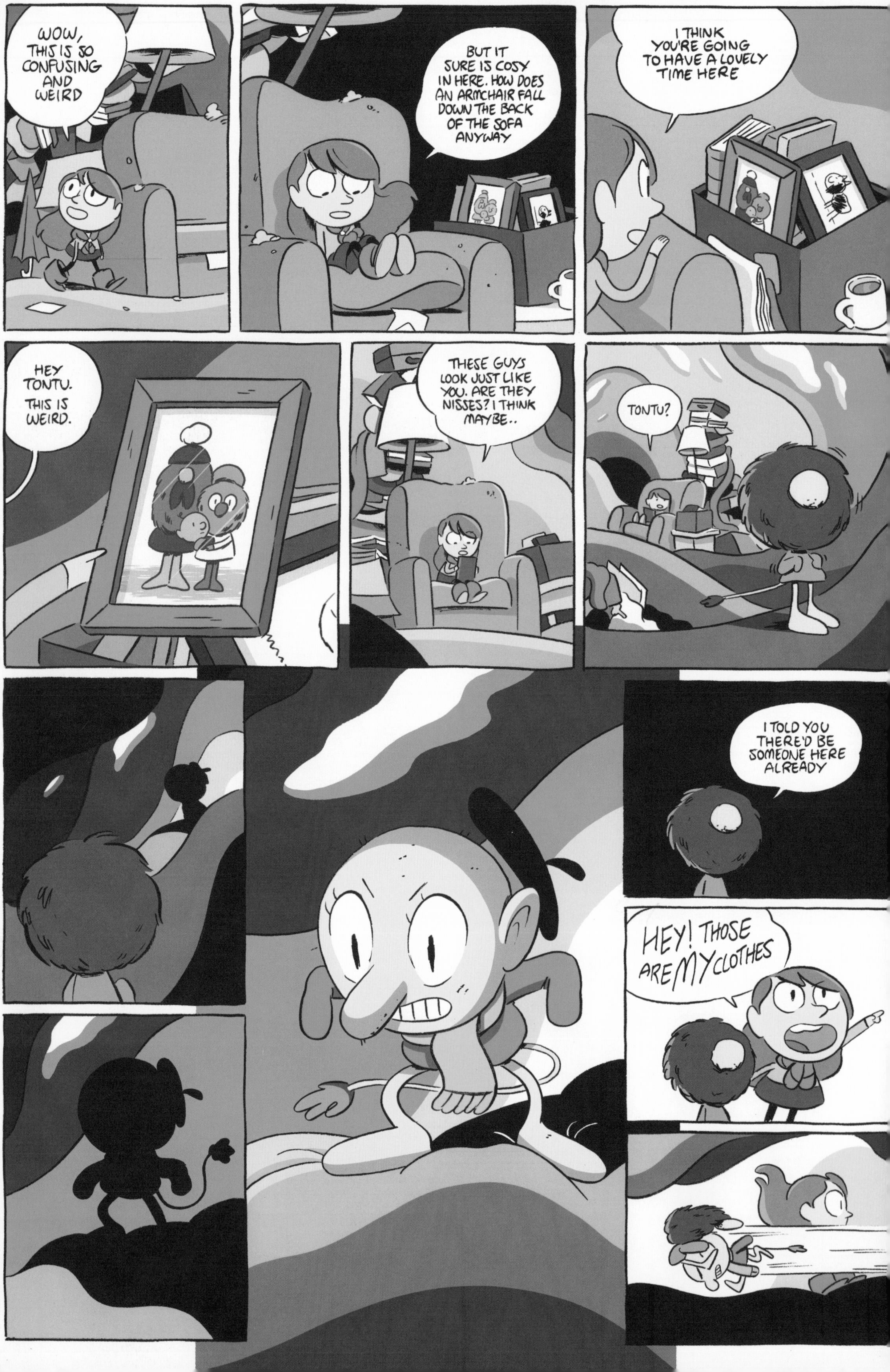
WOW, THIS IS SO CONFUSING AND WEIRD
BUT IT SURE IS COSY IN HERE. HOW DOES AN ARMCHAIR FALL DOWN THE BACK OF THE SOFA ANYWAY
I THINK YOU'RE GOING TO HAVE A LOVELY TIME HERE
HEY TONTU. THIS IS WEIRD.
THESE GUYS LOOK JUST LIKE YOU. ARE THEY NISSES? I THINK MAYBE..
TONTU?
I TOLD YOU THERE'D BE SOMEONE HERE ALREADY
HEY! THOSE ARE MY CLOTHES

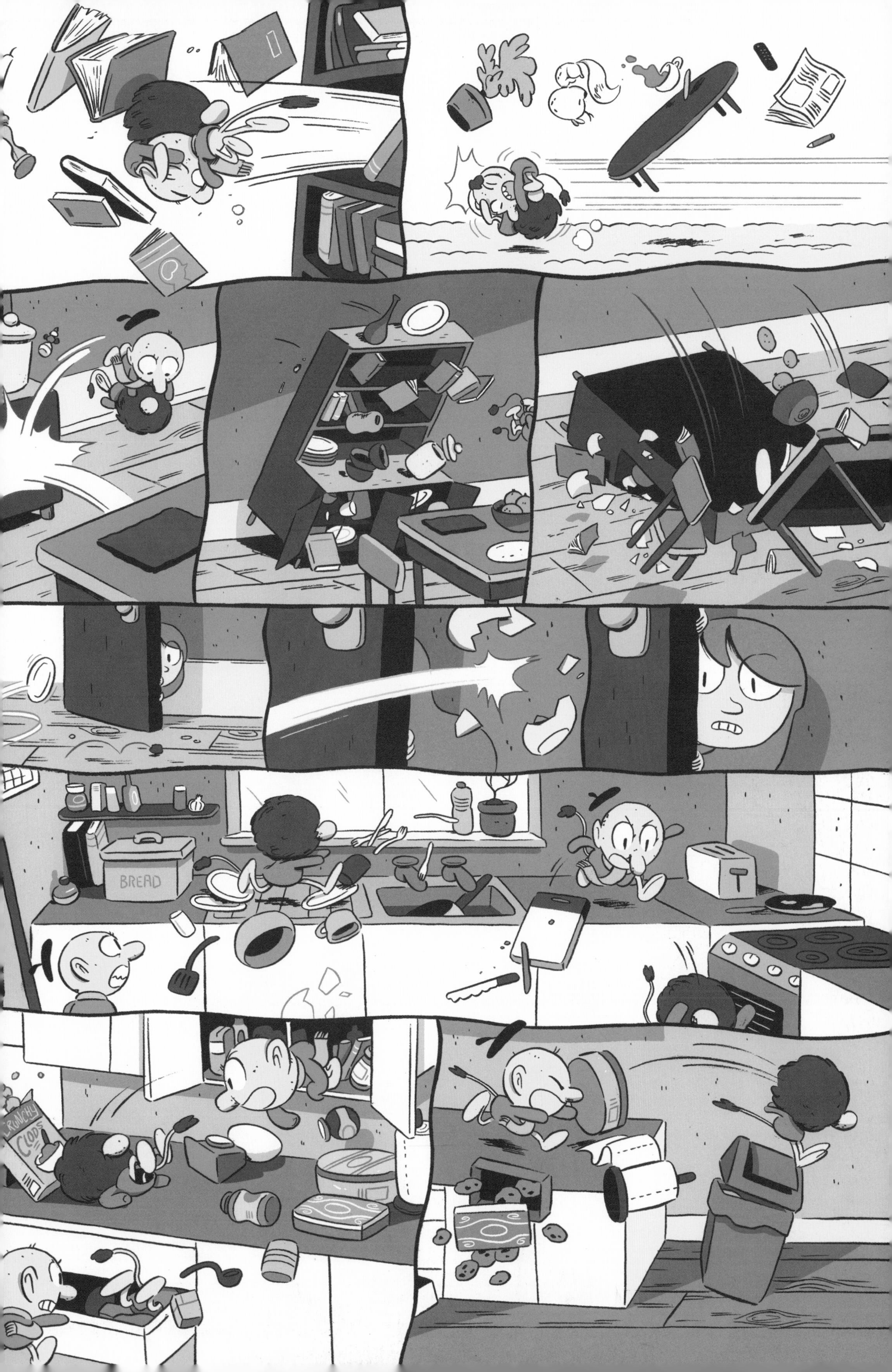
BREAD
CRUNCHY
CLODS

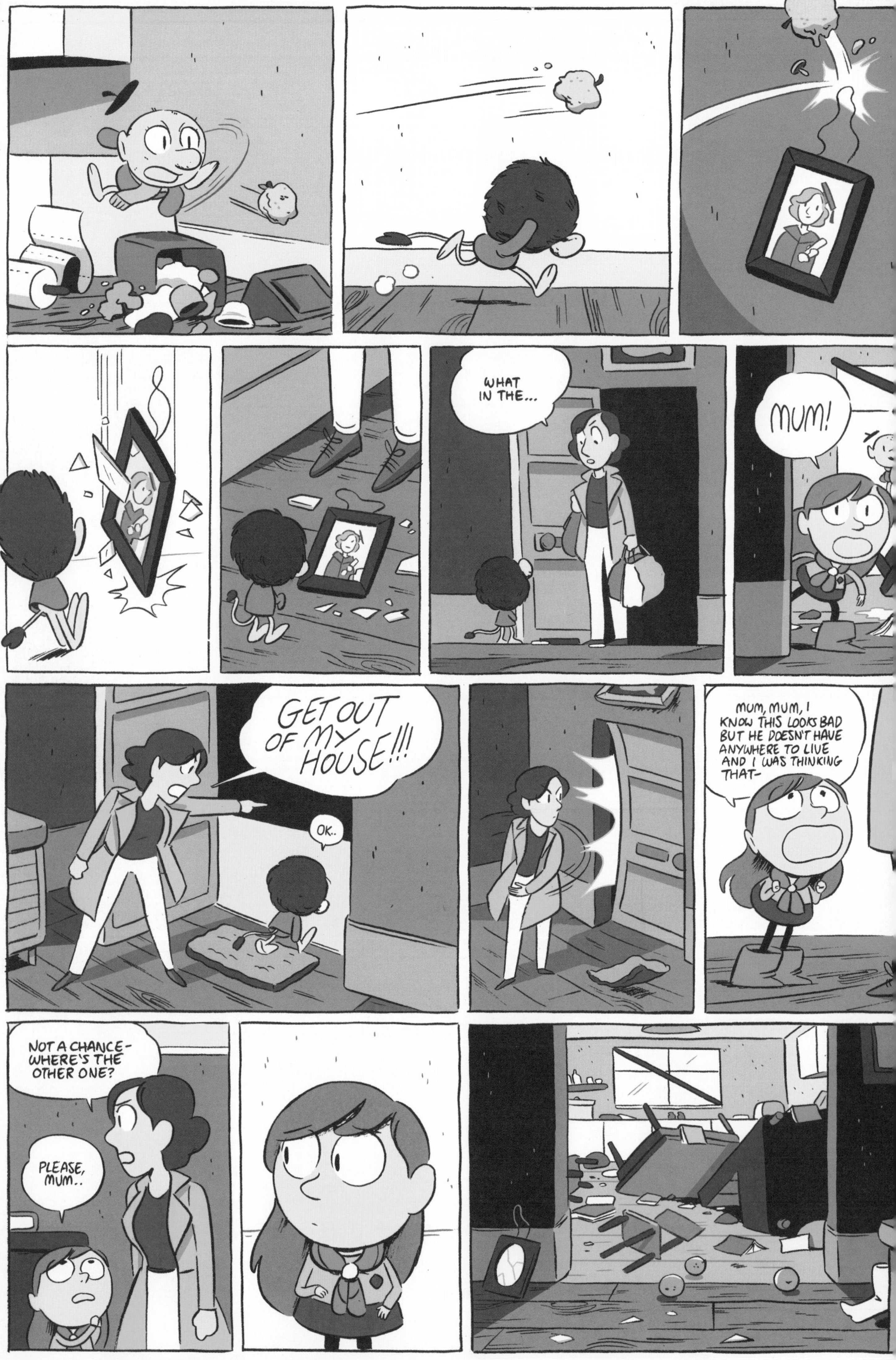
WHAT IN THE...
MUM!
GET OUT OF MY HOUSE!!!
OK..
MUM, MUM, I KNOW THIS LOOKS BAD BUT HE DOESN'T HAVE ANYWHERE TO LIVE AND I WAS THINKING THAT-
NOT A CHANCE- WHERE'S THE OTHER ONE?
PLEASE, MUM..

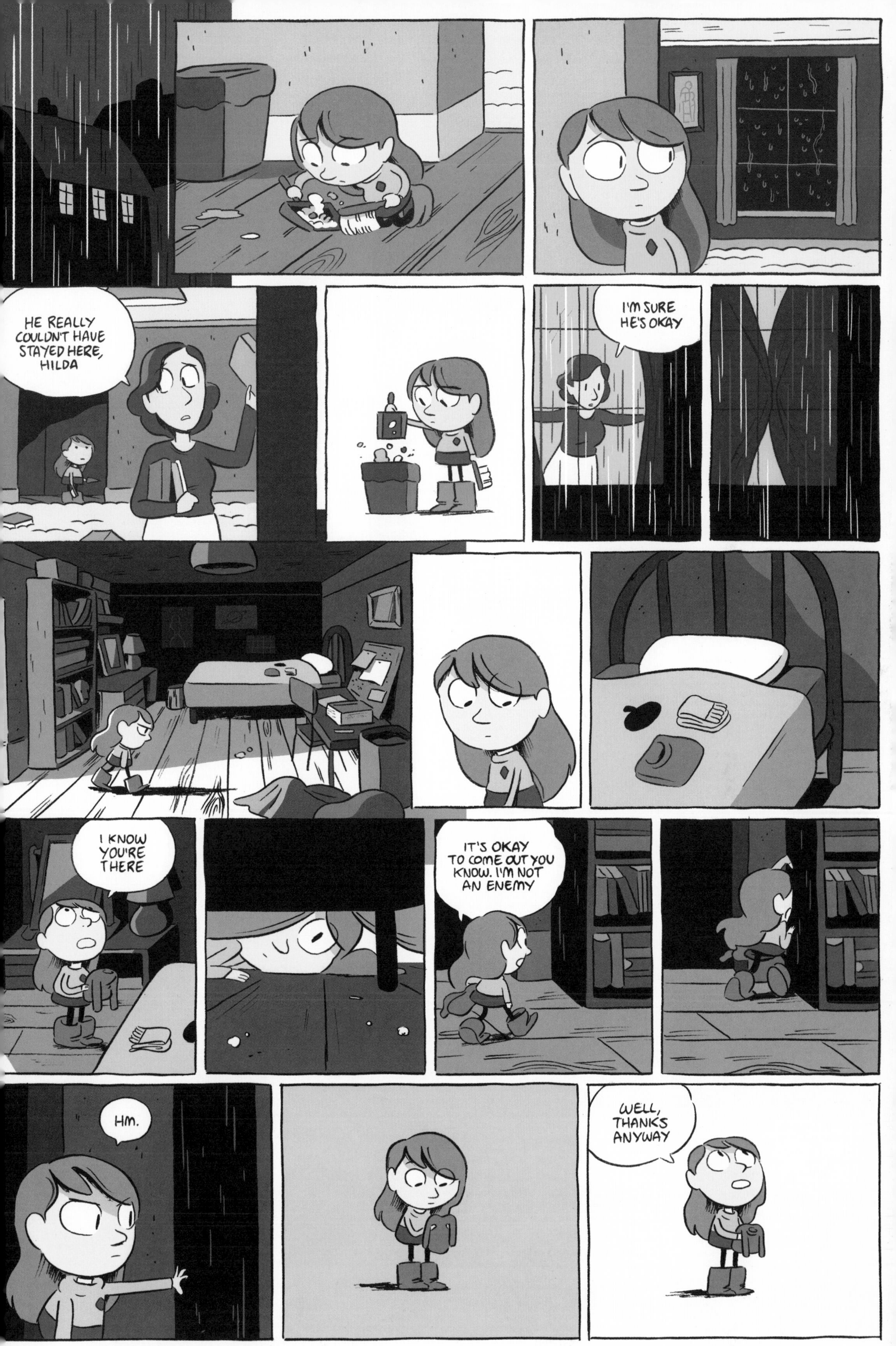
HE REALLY COULDN'T HAVE STAYED HERE, HILDA
I'M SURE HE'S OKAY
I KNOW YOU'RE THERE
IT'S OKAY TO COME OUT YOU KNOW. I'M NOT AN ENEMY
HM.
WELL, THANKS ANYWAY

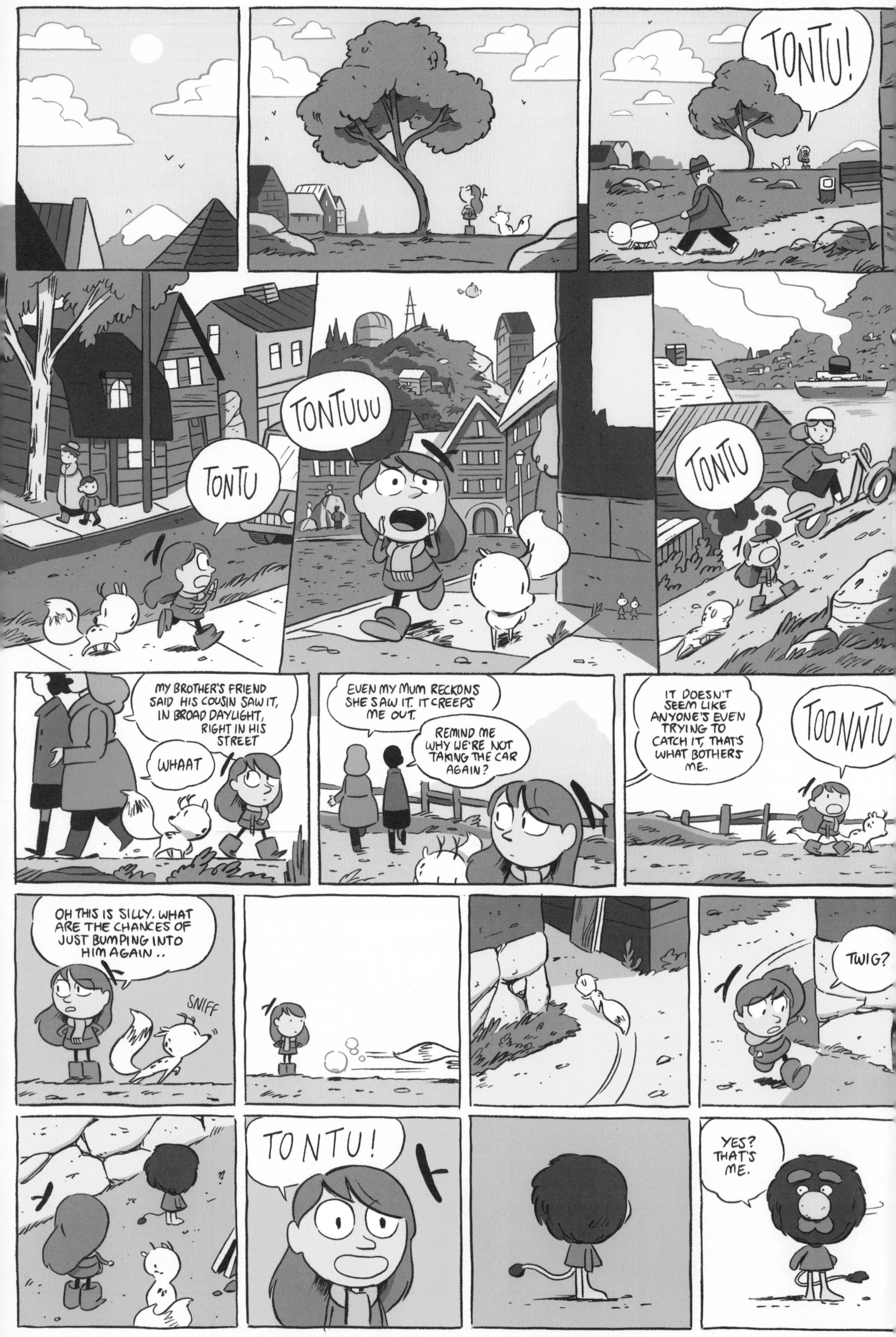

TONTU!
TONTU
TONTUUU
TONTU
MY BROTHER'S FRIEND SAID HIS COUSIN SAW IT, IN BROAD DAYLIGHT, RIGHT IN HIS STREET
WHAAT
EVEN MY MUM RECKONS SHE SAW IT. IT CREEPS ME OUT.
REMIND ME WHY WE'RE NOT TAKING THE CAR AGAIN?
IT DOESN'T SEEM LIKE ANYONE'S EVEN TRYING TO CATCH IT, THAT'S WHAT BOTHERS ME.
TOONNTU
OH THIS IS SILLY. WHAT ARE THE CHANCES OF JUST BUMPING INTO HIM AGAIN..
SNIFF
TWIG?
TONTU!
YES? THAT'S ME.

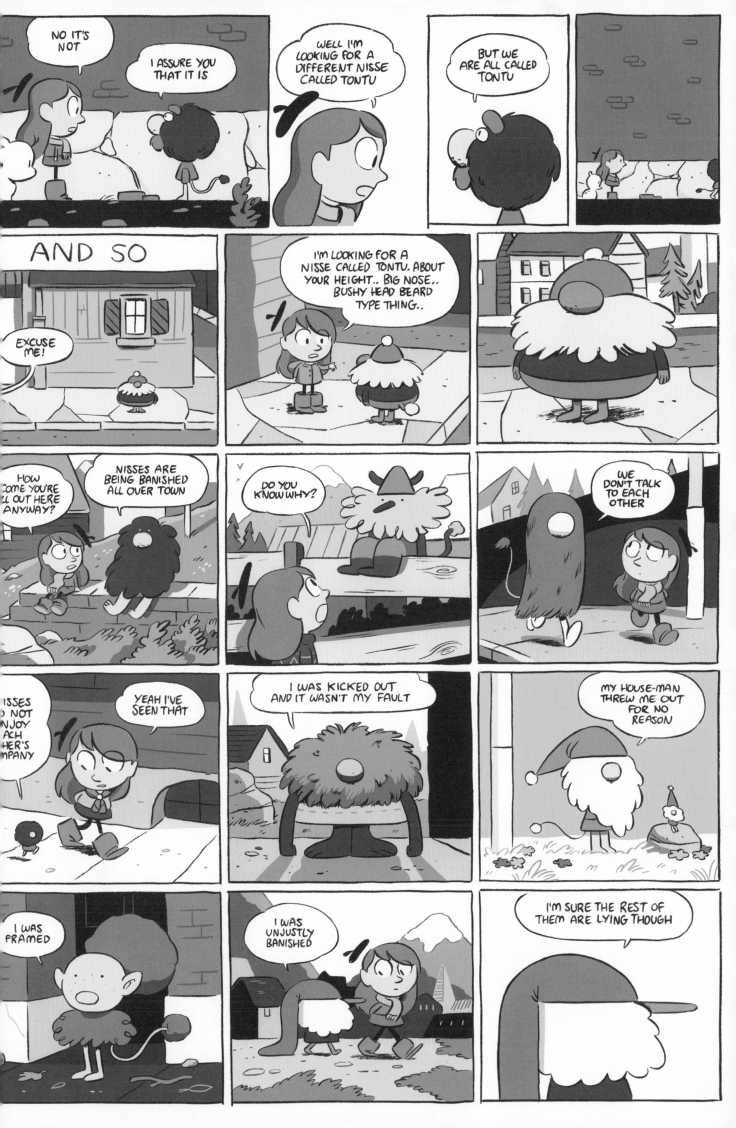

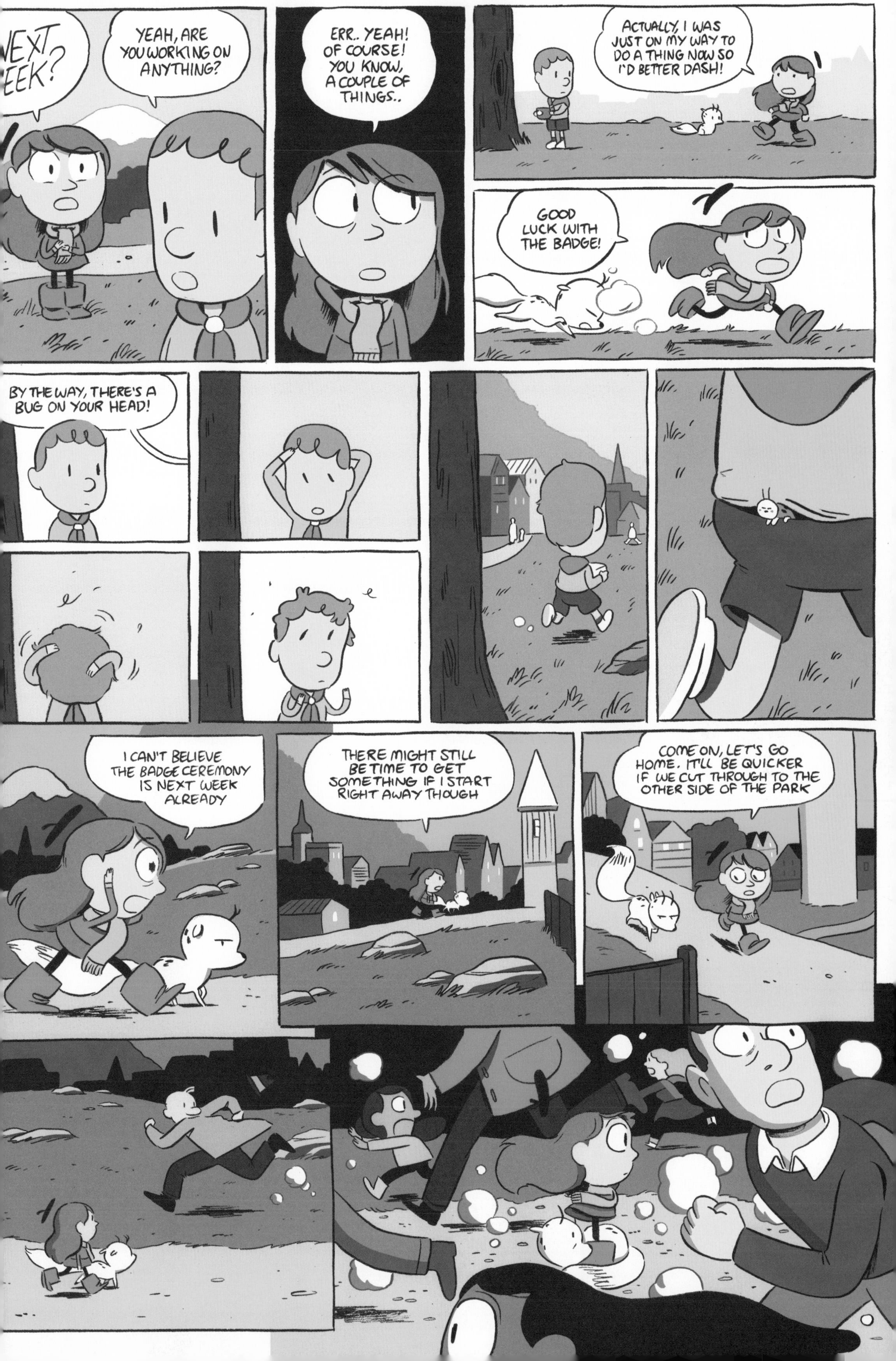
NEXT WEEK?
YEAH, ARE YOU WORKING ON ANYTHING?
ERR.. YEAH! OF COURSE! YOU KNOW, A COUPLE OF THINGS..
ACTUALLY, I WAS JUST ON MY WAY TO DO A THING NOW SO I'D BETTER DASH!
GOOD LUCK WITH THE BADGE!
BY THE WAY, THERE'S A BUG ON YOUR HEAD!
I CAN'T BELIEVE THE BADGE CEREMONY IS NEXT WEEK ALREADY
THERE MIGHT STILL BE TIME TO GET SOMETHING IF I START RIGHT AWAY THOUGH
COME ON, LET'S GO HOME. IT'LL BE QUICKER IF WE CUT THROUGH TO THE OTHER SIDE OF THE PARK

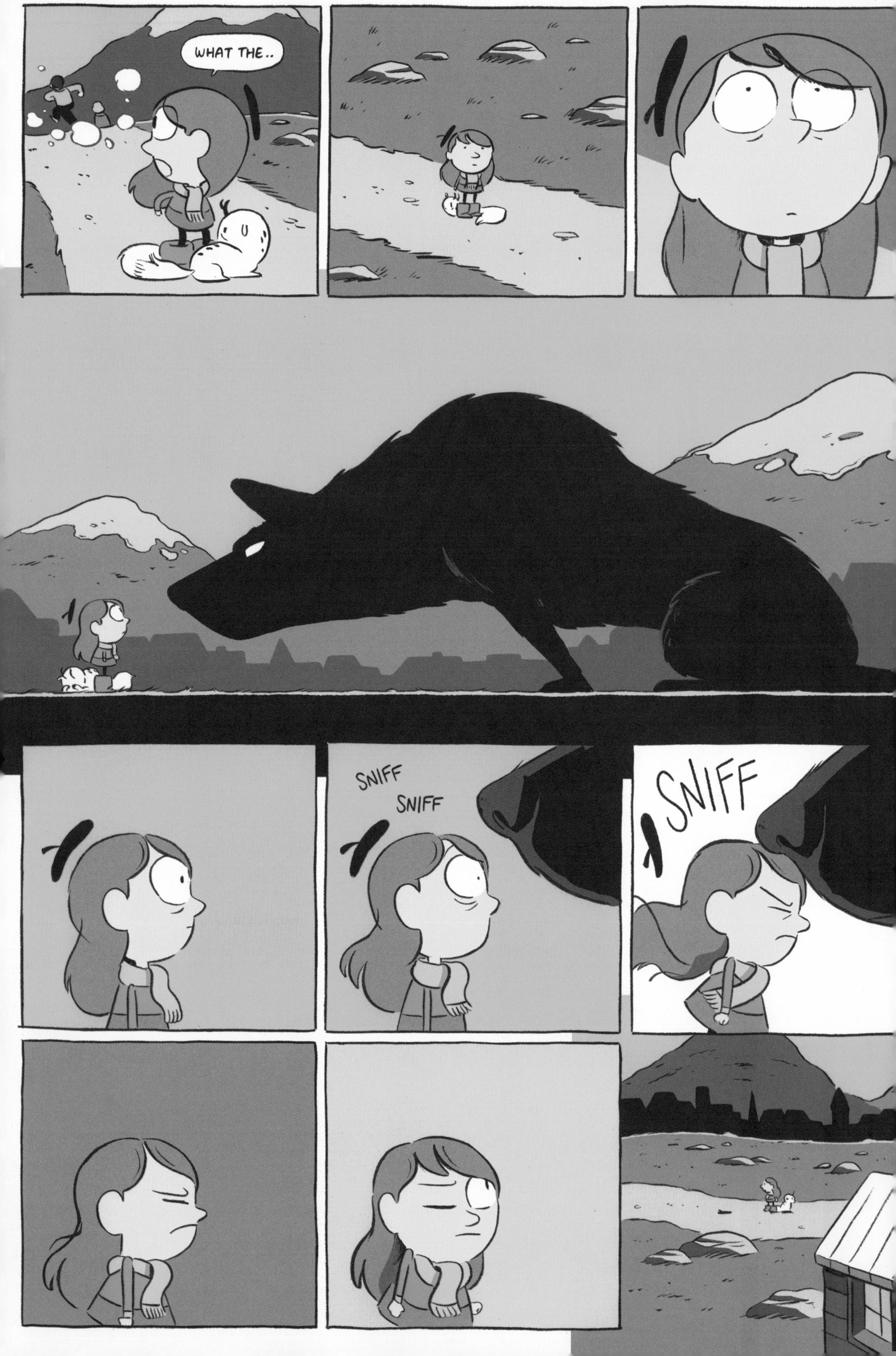
WHAT THE..
SNIFF
SNIFF
SNIFF

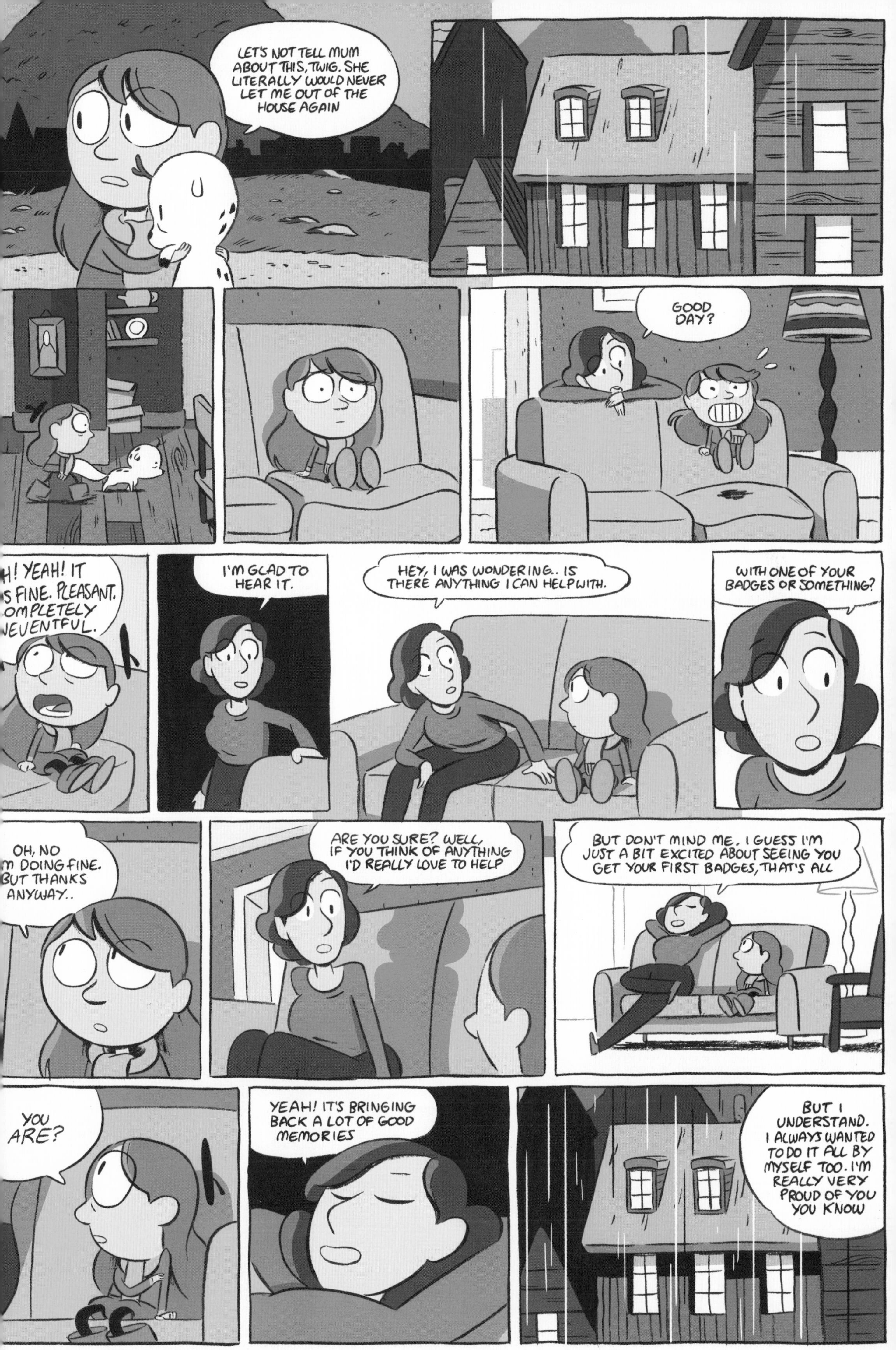
LET'S NOT TELL MUM ABOUT THIS, TWIG. SHE LITERALLY WOULD NEVER LET ME OUT OF THE HOUSE AGAIN
GOOD DAY?
H! YEAH! IT S FINE. PLEASANT. OMPLETELY NEVENTFUL.
I'M GLAD TO HEAR IT.
HEY, I WAS WONDERING.. IS THERE ANYTHING I CAN HELP WITH.
WITH ONE OF YOUR BADGES OR SOMETHING?
OH, NO M DOING FINE. BUT THANKS ANYWAY..
ARE YOU SURE? WELL, IF YOU THINK OF ANYTHING I'D REALLY LOVE TO HELP
BUT DON'T MIND ME. I GUESS I'M JUST A BIT EXCITED ABOUT SEEING YOU GET YOUR FIRST BADGES, THAT'S ALL
YOU ARE?
YEAH! IT'S BRINGING BACK A LOT OF GOOD MEMORIES
BUT I UNDERSTAND. I ALWAYS WANTED TO DO IT ALL BY MYSELF TOO. I'M REALLY VERY PROUD OF YOU YOU KNOW

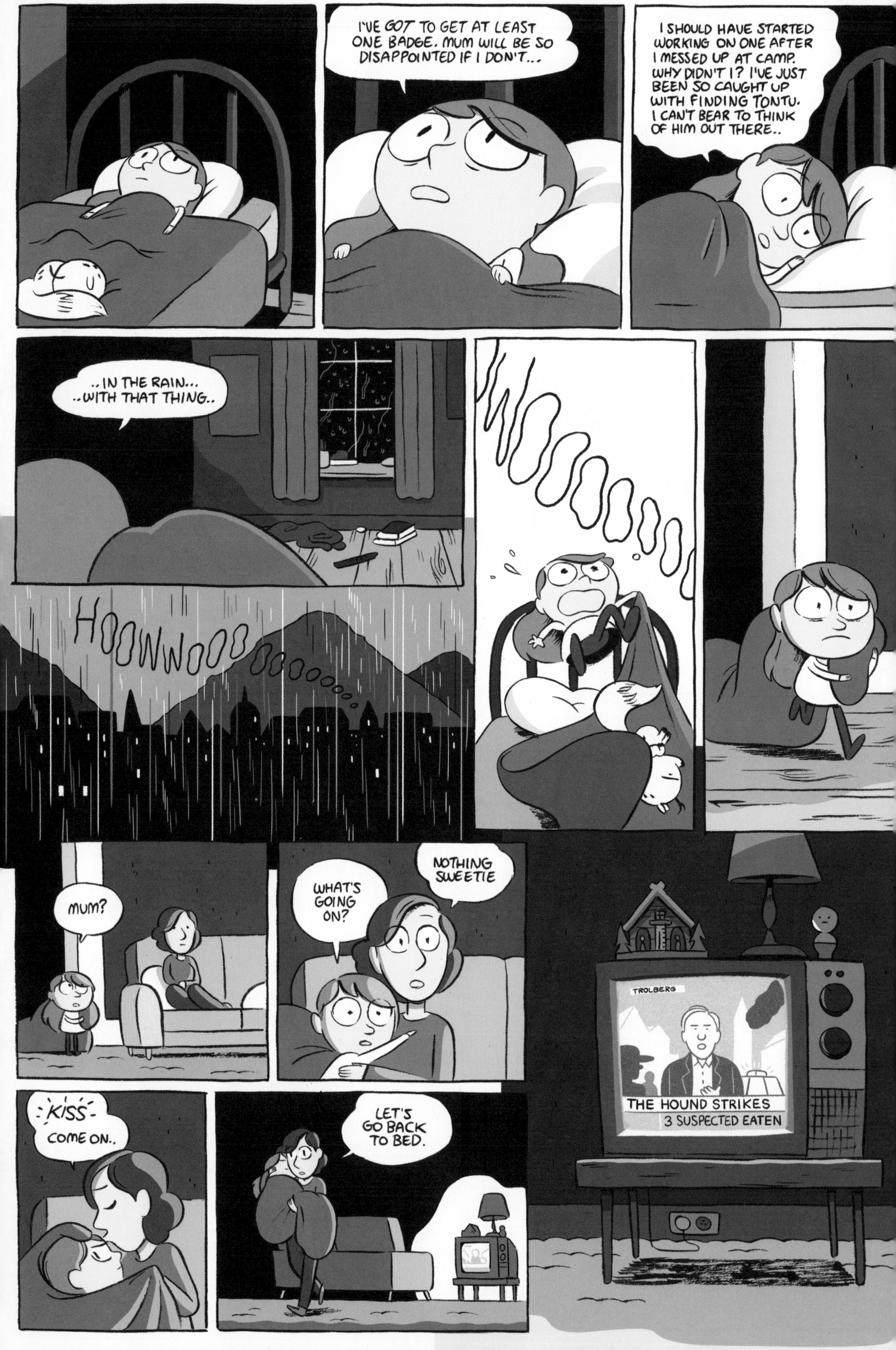
I'VE GOT TO GET AT LEAST ONE BADGE. MUM WILL BE SO DISAPPOINTED IF I DON'T...
I SHOULD HAVE STARTED WORKING ON ONE AFTER I MESSED UP AT CAMP. WHY DIDN'T I? I'VE JUST BEEN SO CAUGHT UP WITH FINDING TONTU. I CAN'T BEAR TO THINK OF HIM OUT THERE..
..IN THE RAIN... ..WITH THAT THING..
HOOWNOOOOOOOOOO
WHOOOOOOOOO
MUM?
WHAT'S GOING ON?
NOTHING SWEETIE
TROLBERG
THE HOUND STRIKES
3 SUSPECTED EATEN
KISS
COME ON..
LET'S GO BACK TO BED.

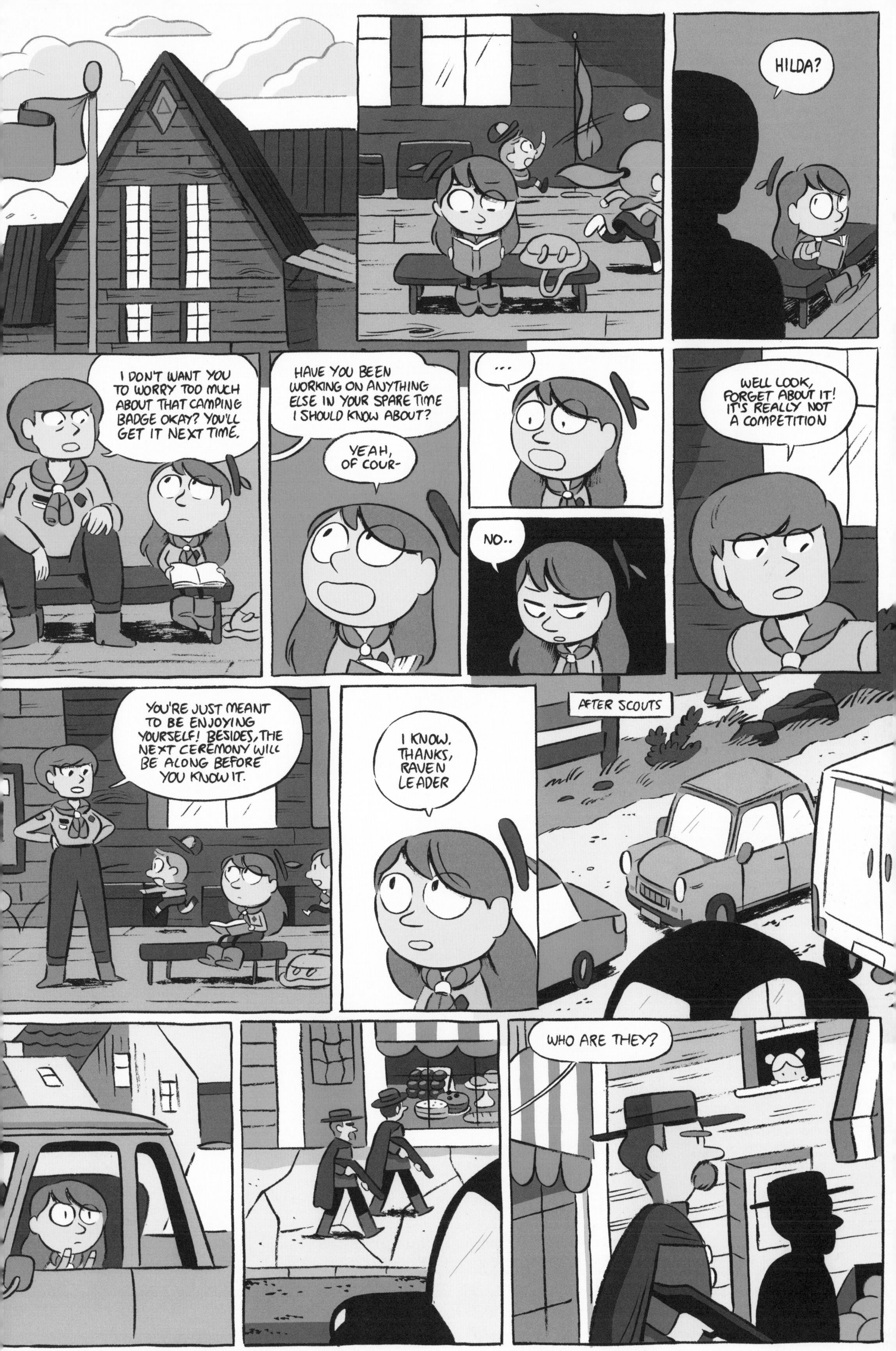
HILDA?
I DON'T WANT YOU TO WORRY TOO MUCH ABOUT THAT CAMPING BADGE OKAY? YOU'LL GET IT NEXT TIME.
HAVE YOU BEEN WORKING ON ANYTHING ELSE IN YOUR SPARE TIME I SHOULD KNOW ABOUT?
YEAH, OF COUR-
...
NO..
WELL LOOK, FORGET ABOUT IT! IT'S REALLY NOT A COMPETITION
YOU'RE JUST MEANT TO BE ENJOYING YOURSELF! BESIDES, THE NEXT CEREMONY WILL BE ALONG BEFORE YOU KNOW IT.
I KNOW. THANKS, RAVEN LEADER
AFTER SCOUTS
WHO ARE THEY?

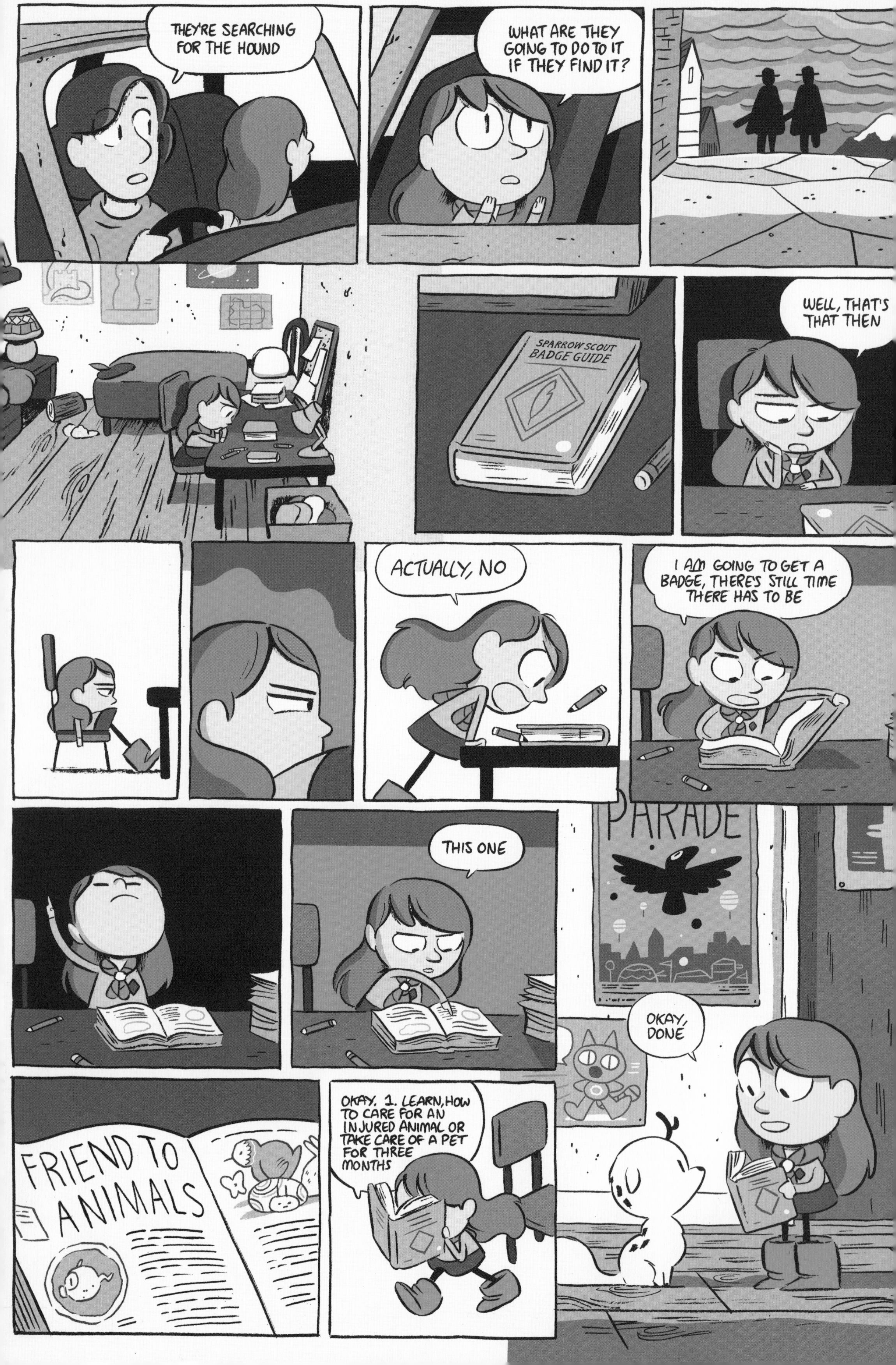
THEY'RE SEARCHING FOR THE HOUND
WHAT ARE THEY GOING TO DO TO IT IF THEY FIND IT?
SPARROW SCOUT BADGE GUIDE
WELL, THAT'S THAT THEN
ACTUALLY, NO
I AM GOING TO GET A BADGE, THERE'S STILL TIME THERE HAS TO BE
THIS ONE
PARADE
OKAY, DONE
FRIEND TO ANIMALS
OKAY. 1. LEARN HOW TO CARE FOR AN INJURED ANIMAL OR TAKE CARE OF A PET FOR THREE MONTHS

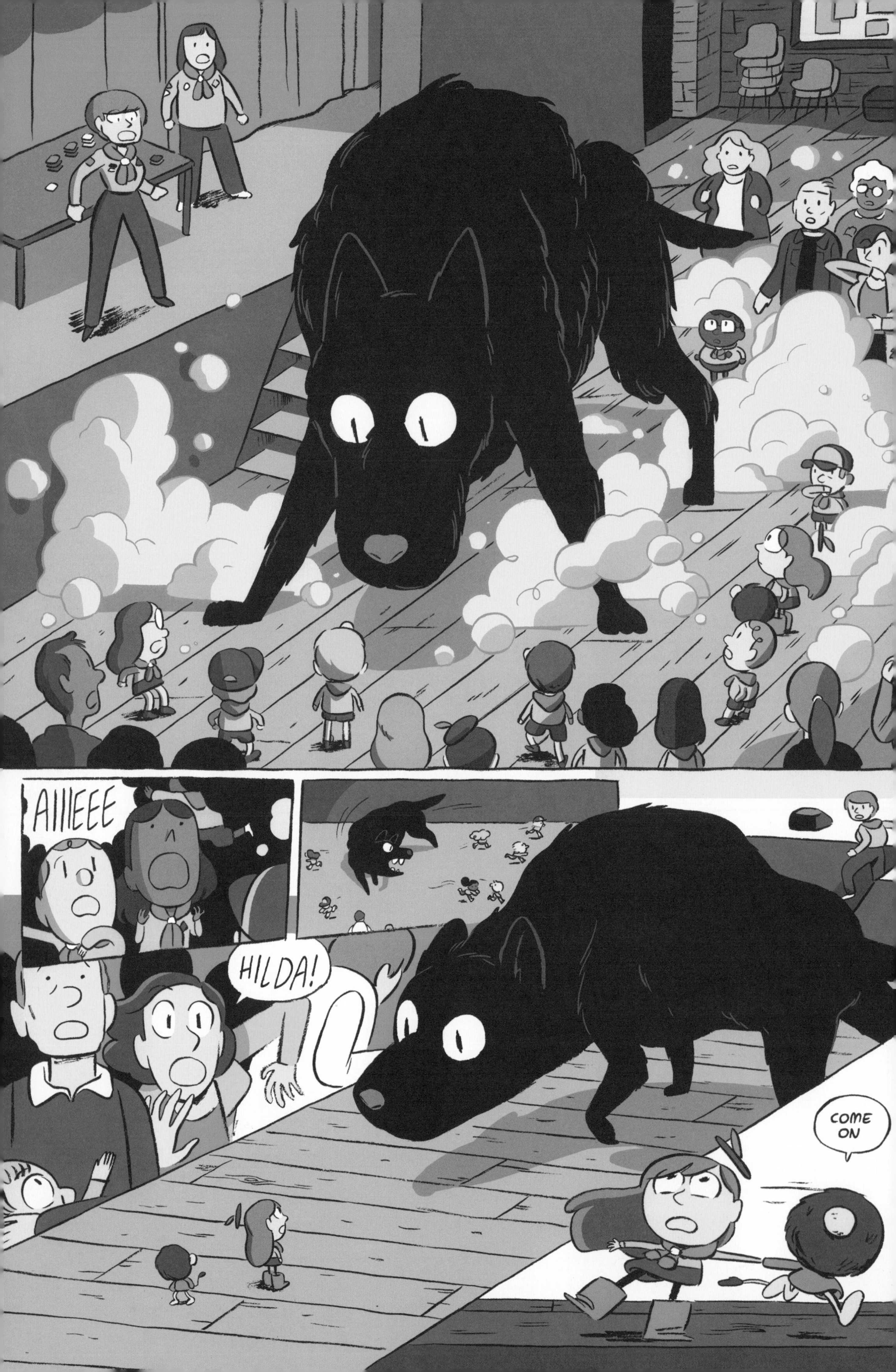
AIIIEEE
HILDA!
COME ON

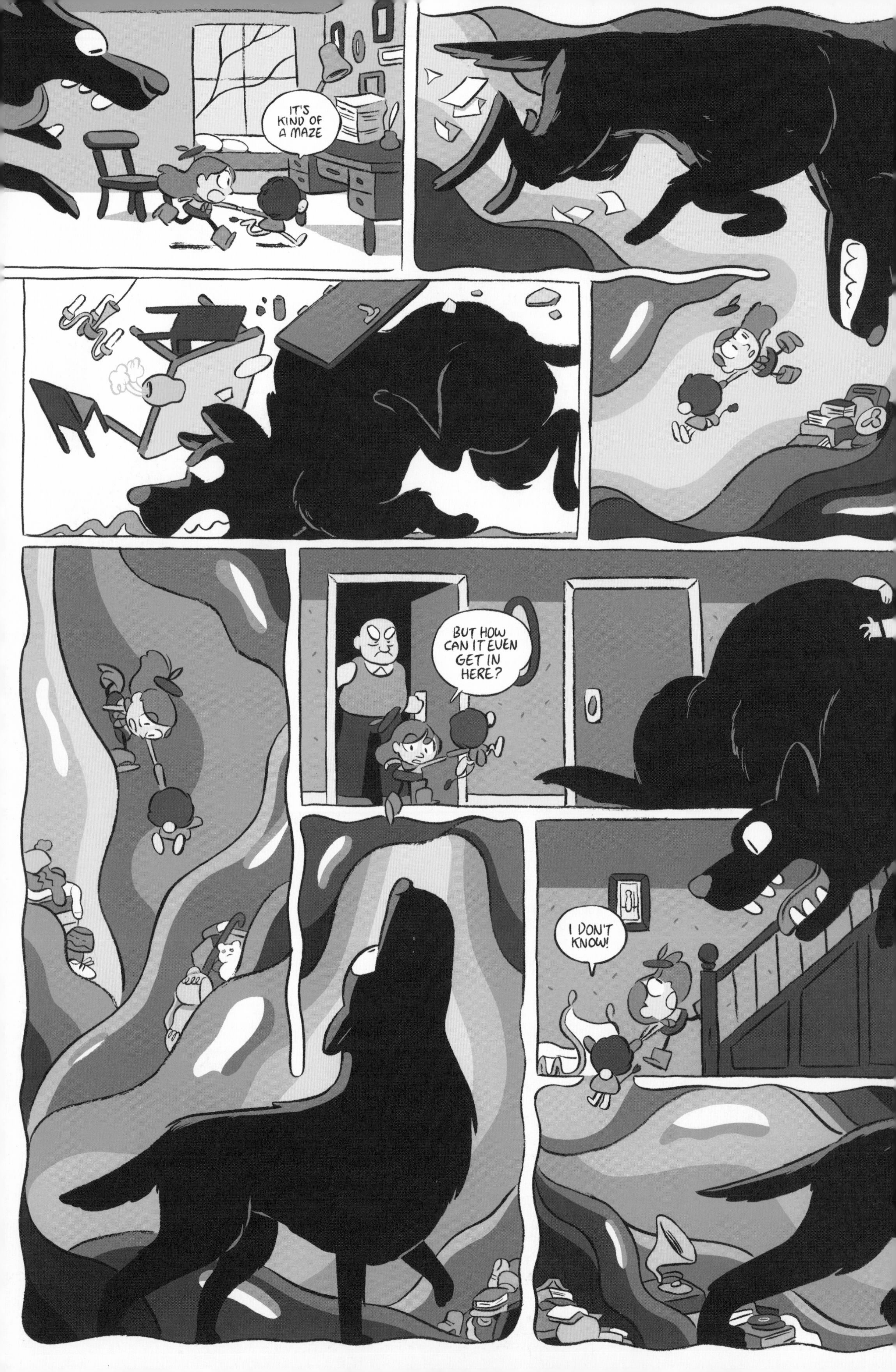
IT'S KIND OF A MAZE
BUT HOW CAN IT EVEN GET IN HERE?
I DON'T KNOW!

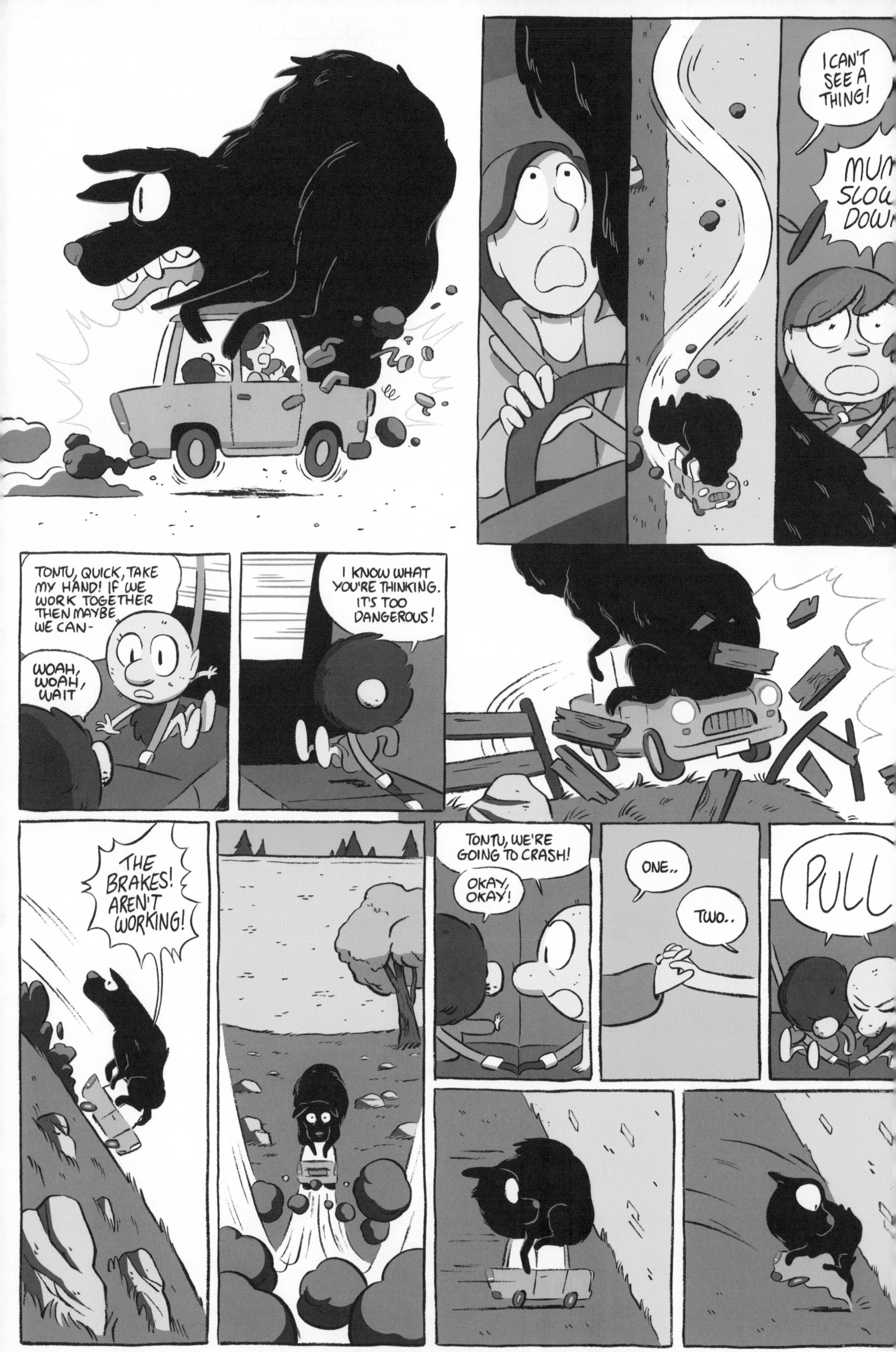

I CAN'T SEE A THING!
MUM SLOW DOWN
TONTU, QUICK, TAKE MY HAND! IF WE WORK TOGETHER THEN MAYBE WE CAN-
WOAH, WOAH, WAIT
I KNOW WHAT YOU'RE THINKING. IT'S TOO DANGEROUS!
THE BRAKES! AREN'T WORKING!
TONTU, WE'RE GOING TO CRASH!
OKAY, OKAY!
ONE..
TWO..
PULL

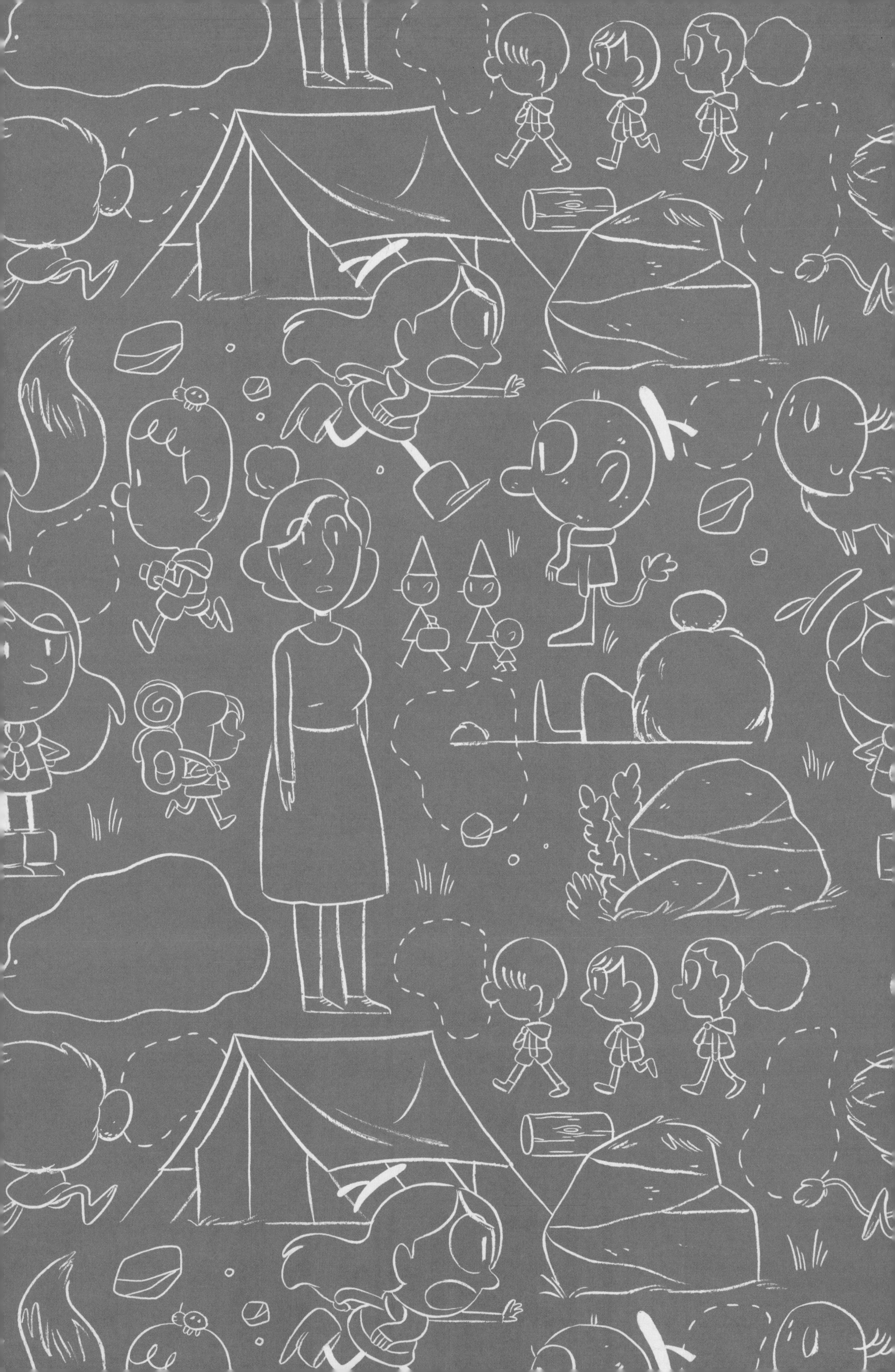